# Soldier Mom

Also by Alice Mead

Alice Mead

# Soldier Mom

A Sunburst Book

Farrar, Straus and Giroux

The author gratefully acknowledges Dr. Steven L. Burg, Professor of Politics, Brandeis University, for his critical reading of the manuscript.

Distributed in Canada by Douglas & McIntyre Ltd.
Printed in the United States of America
First edition, 1999
Sunburst edition, 2009
10  9  8  7  6  5  4  3  2  1

Library of Congress Cataloging-in-Publication Data
Mead, Alice.

 Soldier mom / Alice Mead.— 1st ed.

  p.  cm.

 Summary: Eleven-year-old Jasmyn gets a different perspective on life when her mother is sent to Saudi Arabia at the beginning of the Persian Gulf War, leaving her and her baby half brother behind in Maine in the care of her mother's boyfriend.

 ISBN-13: 978-0-374-40029-3 (pbk.)

 ISBN-10: 0-374-40029-6 (pbk.)

 1. Persian Gulf War, 1991—United States—Juvenile fiction.  [1. Persian Gulf War, 1991—United States—Fiction.  2. Mothers and daughters—Fiction. 3. Single-parent family—Fiction.]  I. Title.

PZ7.M47887So  1999
[Fic]—dc21

                                                                98-55434

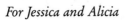

*For Jessica and Alicia*

In 1991, America went to war in the Persian Gulf. On January 16, George H. W. Bush ordered the United States and its allies to launch a massive air strike against Iraq. This was followed in February by a four-day land war fought with tanks. The Persian Gulf War, called Operation Desert Storm, was America's first war fought with a volunteer army.

In August 1990, long before the missiles were fired, President Bush made the decision to call up a large number of military reserve forces. The heavy use of reserve troops meant that many soldiers were living at home with their families, instead of on army bases, at the time they were mobilized.

War has always been disruptive of family life, but this one had a special impact on women soldiers and their children. Approximately 37,000 women were sent to Desert Storm. Among the soldiers were 16,300 single parents, as well as 1,200 military couples who had children. Especially at the beginning of mobilization, soldiers were summoned on extremely short notice, leaving their children without suitable long-term care.

# Soldier Mom

# 1

"Jas!"

"Yeah. Coming."

"Jas! It's a quarter to six."

"Hold on, will ya? Jeez. Can't you let me find my sneakers? It's not like Coach is going to start without me or anything."

I hop into the kitchen, trying to pull on a sneaker and then tie it standing up. My ten-month-old baby brother, Andrew, stands clinging to the seat of the kitchen chair. Every time I hop, he laughs.

Mom bends over and rubs her nose on his. "What's so funny? Huh? What's so funny?"

Andrew laughs harder. He has a great big belly laugh that my mom and I love to hear.

I collapse into a chair to put on my other size 9½ sneaker. Beginning last year, in sixth grade, kids at school, egged on by Shawn Doucette, called me "Bigfoot." At first I didn't mind, but after a whole year of it, I'd had enough.

I tug at my white athletic socks. I'm wearing dark

green shiny shorts and a baggy dull gray tank top that says "Alcatraz Federal Penitentiary" on it. The shirt belongs to my best friend, Danielle Roberge, but I borrowed it, maybe forever. I stand up and brush myself off.

"There. I'm ready. How do I look?"

"That shirt is awful," says Mom, sighing.

I look down at it. "Yeah." I grin. "I know."

"Your hair's a mess, too. Want me to braid it?"

"Nah. It's just a tryout for Pre-season League. No big deal, Mom. Relax."

"I am feeling nervous. Maybe there's a thunderstorm coming."

Thunderstorms are rare where we live, along the Maine coast. The cold Atlantic air breaks up the puffy white towers of thunderhead clouds that drift across the mountains from New Hampshire on late summer afternoons. Today, August 2, a stiff afternoon breeze has been blowing up from the cove. Mom steps out on the back deck, carrying Andrew on her hip.

"It's gusty, Jasmyn. Make sure you shut the back door tightly," she adds.

"Okay."

"I don't want it blowing open."

"I'm eleven, Mom. I think I can shut the door by myself."

I live with my mother and little brother and sometimes Mom's boyfriend, Jake, although he's in and out, in a coastal Maine town called Stroudwater. Stroudwater may be small, but there's nothing small about its dedication to schoolboy and schoolgirl basketball. Making the seventh-grade team is the first big step on the path to high school varsity. Everybody knows it. Half the town will probably show up at tonight's tryouts. Every girl's dad will be there, except mine.

We hop in the car, a slightly rusty beige 1985 Oldsmobile. Duct tape patches hold together a perfectly decent red vinyl interior that's ripped here and there.

The engine catches. Mom tromps quickly on the gas, but the engine stalls anyway. I smell gasoline. The engine has flooded. Ho-hum. The seconds are ticking by.

We watch the Parnells, the people next door, water their garden. Now Mrs. Parnell is cleaning their above-ground pool. One day, Danielle and I found a couple of frogs floating around in there. We couldn't figure out how they jumped thirty-six inches into the air to get over the side. The frogs were dead, because they can't live in chlorine.

If the Parnells weren't so grouchy, maybe Danielle and I could be floating around in the pool instead of frogs. We've asked them a couple of times, but they've never said yes. Just when you think you are their permanent enemies, however, they smile and act nice and give you zucchinis.

Now I'm nervous. It's much too late to walk. "Want me to take my bike?"

"Not yet. Hey," Mom says, "you think I'm a quitter? Huh? When the going gets tough—"

"No!" I yelp, and clap my hands over my ears. The saying is "When the going gets tough, the tough get going." I cannot tell you how many times I've heard that. It's one of those boot camp things.

My mom went through six weeks of basic training at Lackland Air Force Base in Texas. She is not a quitter. She stays in great shape, jogging, working out, lifting weights. She can do anything her country asks of her. Right now she's working for the army as a supply coordinator at an office in Portland.

My mom is tall. My dad, an air force pilot in Japan, is tall. I have tallness in me, waiting to come out. I am a big kid. Everyone says I will be huge because of my long legs and big feet. I can dribble between my knees. That's how I make my move, my under-the-basket, between-the-knees-dribble, turn, fake, and layup shot.

As we wait for the gasoline to calm down inside the carburetor, Mom sighs and says something really strange. "Don't ever think you're more special than other people, that you don't have to work as hard or suffer as much."

"Huh?" I look at her. What's that supposed to mean? Suddenly I feel desperate to get to tryouts.

Mom's still staring at Mr. Parnell. He's digging up potatoes. Now Mrs. Parnell is bringing over the wheelbarrow. From a distance, they look cuddly and cute, like the apple dolls at the church craft fair.

They live to our east, right at the top of the cliff above Spar Cove, in a big old farmhouse they can't take proper care of anymore. On the other side, the house faces the channel and Moorhead Island.

"Oh, I don't know. Don't take being in Pre-season for granted, I guess. Remember to work at it every day."

"Yeah. Well, yeah. I will. Besides, if I don't, you'll remind me, right?"

She doesn't answer. Just looks down at her lap. Something is up. This is absolutely not normal.

"Right?" I ask again.

Mr. Parnell is standing up now, staring at his tomato plants.

"Come on, Mom. Let's go. Please? We'll be late. Danielle thinks Coach is going to pick me for captain. If you're team captain, you have to help set up and put equipment away at the end."

Mom turns the key again. The engine starts. We back slowly out of the driveway. As we start forward, the car gives two big lurches, but then, thank God, the engine catches for real. "Mom, hurry, okay?"

"Quiet!" she snaps at me. "Just be quiet!"

I shrink down in my seat. Wow. It's not like her at all to lose her temper like that. She usually warns me first. What on earth is up?

# 2

Mom says in a calmer voice, "I'm sorry, Jas, for yelling at you."

"That's okay."

Thinking back, I realize Mom started acting weird during the five o'clock news. Was it the weather? I try to remember what the weatherman said. Nothing. No clouds today, sunshine all the way to Idaho. How could Mom even think about a thunderstorm?

"I know. Are you having PMS?"

She bursts out laughing. "No. That's enough, okay? I'm fine."

From his car seat in back, Andrew lets out a holler.

"Jas, can you see what he wants?"

I whip around. "What, Andrew?"

He points. There, on the floor, is his favorite blanket, Binky.

I unlatch my seat belt and lean over the seat to reach for it.

"Jas!" Mom yells. "What are you doing?"

"Getting his blanket. You just told me to."

I hand Binky to Andrew, and he grins and clasps it to his chest.

"So I did," Mom mutters.

"Come on, Mom, you can tell me," I say. "Did you have a fight with Jake?"

My mom and I talk to each other this way. Straight out. No secrets. Jake is Mom's boyfriend and Andrew's dad. They've been engaged for two years, but still aren't married. My mom keeps getting cold feet. Whatever they decide is fine. Jake has nothing to do with me.

"No, I didn't have a fight with Jake," Mom says.

"Then you think I won't make the team? I will. I promise I'll do a good job out there. I'll hustle, okay?"

"Remember on the five o'clock news tonight, when they showed a tiny country called Kuwait?" she asks.

"No."

"They showed some camels and oil wells and then tanks?"

"Not really."

Mom sighs.

We park the big, old car. Mom gets out and reaches into the back to drag Andrew from his car seat. He weighs a ton.

"Yeah, so what was it about camels?" I ask.

Mom smiles at me. "Nothing. Good luck at tryouts. Come on. I'll race you."

With Andrew on her hip, Mom takes off running across the parking lot. Andrew is laughing in his usual great big chuckling way. And that makes me laugh, slowing me down. Besides, I'm a little worried about getting a cramp in my side before tryouts. So Mom and Andrew win.

She turns at the door and yells, "I win! I win!"

I yell back, "I let you! I let you!"

Inside, the hallway is cool and dark, but it's also humid, from being closed up all summer. Everything smells like floor polish and fresh paint. That's about all our school gets—cleaned and patched up, never anything new.

There is one exception to our school's worn-out condition. The gym floor is almost brand-new.

"Jas!"

"Hey, Mr. Campbell!"

"Call me Coach."

"Oh, yeah. Hi, Coach."

Coach Campbell is paunchier than you might think would be good for a basketball coach. He is mostly bald. And he has a slight limp from too much knee surgery. He always wears a whistle.

Most of the girls are already there, including Bridget O'Donnell and Amy Forest, the little sheep who follows her everywhere. Bridget and Amy have the newest ball and have claimed one of the baskets for their own; they spend most of the warm-up time telling the other seven girls they can't use it. Bridget is wearing a brand-new Red Star Hoop Camp T-shirt with "MVP" stenciled on the back. What a show-off! Red Star costs a ton of money. There's no way Mom could afford to send me.

"It's ten after six, folks. Start some warm-up laps, everybody. Let's go!" Coach claps his hands together.

I hop right up and get going. My mom taught me not to skimp on the small stuff, but to go all out, big or small. And soon I'm in the lead, even though I'm not running fast. I'm concentrating.

As I pass the gym lobby doors for the third time, I notice that a large group of grown-ups is talking with my mom. The junior high social studies teacher, Mr. Arthur, is there. So are lots of the parents of the girls who are here.

Mr. Arthur looks very serious. His head is tipped to one side, like a bird looking at a pebble. He's rattling the coins in his pocket and staring at the shiny yellow floor.

"Let's pick up the pace, Jas!" Coach calls out. "Come on, girls. Sprint!"

I can hear Bridget behind me. "Did you see how he singled her out already? He plays such favorites. Besides, it's too hot for sprints," Bridget says to Amy. "I'm going to have my dad tell him we shouldn't have to do sprints if we don't want to."

I suddenly notice she's much too close. Then her foot grazes the heel of my sneaker, so that I stumble forward and nearly fall flat on my face.

"Cut it out, Bridget," I yell, whirling around.

"Ooops, Bigfoot nearly fell!" She laughs. "Maybe you can't run this far 'cause your feet are too heavy."

"Drop dead."

"Is there a problem, girls?" Coach asks.

"No. No problem." We both smile at him.

"Good."

"And by the way, Bridget, don't call me Bigfoot."

If I were the coach, I'd cut Bridget for her attitude. Mom says the most important thing she learned in boot camp was you can do almost anything, no matter how hard. You think you'll never make it, carrying seventy pounds on your back, not getting any sleep, fighting mosquitoes the size of helicopters. You think you're not strong enough and never will be. But you keep trying and trying, and one day, if you keep your mind on it, you'll find you're there.

"Okay, break. Line up on the center line for some passing drills."

"I'll get the balls, Coach." Bridget runs over to the closet and pulls out a big mesh bag of ancient basketballs. The nubbles are worn off.

Suddenly Danielle comes running in. Sorry, she mouths to me from across the gym. Stevie. Again.

Stevie is her younger brother. He's eight and isn't totally normal. He's difficult. He has terrible tantrums and arches his back until you think it'll break.

Danielle has been my best friend since first grade. We are like sisters. Only we look totally different. I have light brown hair and gray eyes. She has dark wavy hair and dark brown eyes. She is part French Canadian and part Greek, and I am nothing interesting.

My hair is long and almost always in a braid, and hers is short and wild. She's great at crouching down low and stealing the ball. And I'm the jumper, the leaper.

Her dad strolls over, his hands in his pockets, to the circle around my mom.

"Jas!" barks Coach. "You with us or against us?"

"With!"

"Let's go, then."

I fall into a rhythm on the court. My feet, my great big bongo Bigfoot feet, are a musical instrument on this wonderful bouncy gym floor. It feels great to run on it. I think there's a layer of rubber under the wood. Or maybe air!

Here to there, here to there. Divide the distance into the right number of steps, get the rhythm. Cross the shiny, silky yellow boards, glossy as a horse in sunlight.

Bounce passes. Kids never look for them. So easy. Bounce past your opponent's foot. Pass to your teammate. Bounce and pass.

And layups. Step, step. Lift and arch your wrist like a piano player lifting music from the flatness of the lying-down keys. That's how I do it. Arch and follow through.

I dribble past the other kids, around them, through them, to make my song. I must make my song. My bongo Bigfoot song. No one can stop me.

I wipe my forehead with a corner of the Alcatraz shirt. I happen to glance up in the bleachers, and I see

Shawn Doucette, sitting in the top row. He waves and yells, "Hi, Jas!"

Then Coach's hand clasps my sweaty shoulder and gives me a little shake. "You're getting better, kid. All the time, you're getting better. You practice a lot this summer?"

Danielle comes over and slides her arm around my waist. The truth is no. I meant to, but I never got around to it. I know he wants me to say yes. To say, "Every day, Coach." It's one of those grown-up questions that come complete with answers. If I say no, he'll be mad. If I say yes, I'm a liar.

"Yes."

"Atta girl."

Danielle looks at me and rolls her eyes, freeing me from my lie. I glance around for my mom. There she is with half the town, it seems. They're all looking at me, and nobody's smiling.

I don't get it. What's wrong?

Shawn comes bounding down the bleachers. "Hey, Bigfoot. You were awesome."

"Yeah? Thanks. Don't call me that," I add automatically. "Shawn, look at the grown-ups. Why are they staring at me?"

"That's weird. I don't know. Maybe they've got the flu. Maybe their underwear is too tight. I find that accounts for a lot of the weirdness typical of grown-ups. Half of 'em have wedgies."

I glare at him.

"Come on. Laugh, Williams. You know you want to."

I'm hot and thirsty, and he's directly in my path to the water fountain. He's intentionally blocking my way.

"Move! I want a drink, you idiot!"

I jog over to the water fountain. Coach is already calling us back to center circle, but everyone's milling around, not paying attention.

Coach gives a shrill blast on his whistle. All the girls run over. Since there are only ten of us here, it doesn't look as if anyone will get cut tonight.

"All right. Listen up. No cuts. During Pre-season I'm gonna be using everybody to see who will play the most in November. Everybody plays for now—the good and the bad. That means bench time for some of you hotshots. You got that, ladies?" He looks at Bridget, and she blushes a little.

"I don't want anybody's parents showing up here, telling me how to coach the team. You miss a practice, you sit out at least half the next game. We have one full week of practice, every afternoon from three till five. The following week, games start: Tuesdays and Thursdays. Three weeks. Don't forget to pick up two jerseys on your way out—one maroon and one white. And I'll see you Monday."

"What a jerk he is," Bridget mutters to Amy. "I told you he hates me. Did you see the way he said that about parents? Next thing you know, he'll make Jas team captain, when I'm the one who went to Red Star, not her."

As we pull our jerseys from the box, Coach yells out.

"Oh, and one more thing. Jasmyn Williams is team captain for Pre-season."

"You see?" Bridget says, loud enough for everyone to hear. "What did I tell you?"

# 3

As soon as we get in the car, I ask, "So what was that huddle all about? Did it have anything to do with a tiny country with camels?"

"Yes, Jas." Mom sighs. "I'll tell you about it when we get home."

That won't take long. Stroudwater is small. Our street is a little over a mile north of the junior high parking lot, a short bike ride. And Andrew's day care is a bit farther down Main, south of the school.

The town center is a crossroads with an old cemetery dating from the Revolutionary War and a Congregational church. Then there's a gas station, a day-care center, post office, two tacky tourist shops, Golly Polly's ice cream, and Ken's Hardware and Handy store. And the schools, of course.

Stroudwater is half on the ocean. Route 1 runs north-south up the middle, and that cuts the whole town in half. Route 1 is for the tourists. The inland half has a smelly paper factory, where Jake works, and a couple of huge sand and gravel pits. And the northern edge still has a few old dairy farms left. That's where Shawn Doucette lives.

I run up the back steps and fling open the screen door. I pull off my sneakers and hot, sweaty gym socks, which I leave in the middle of the living-room floor on my way to my bedroom. The socks are a test for Mom.

I stand in the hall watching, but Mom doesn't even see them. She steps right over them and turns on the TV. That cable news channel again.

"Hey, Mom, there's a movie on tonight. A comedy. Can we watch it after we eat?"

She doesn't answer. All she's done is give Andrew a teething biscuit, which he's already turned to brown mush. He's playing with the boingy phone cord at the same time.

"Mom! Gross! Andrew's eating the phone cord and getting it all gooey."

She doesn't turn her head. I look at the TV, too. It shows a map of a country called Saudi Arabia, then some camels walking next to a flat highway. Camels are the weirdest-looking animals. They're so colorless. With their long, slow legs shimmering in the heat waves, they look as if they're walking on the moon.

"Camels," I say out loud. Then the map returns to the screen.

"Right. See Iraq? Kuwait is below Iraq."

"Yeah. The little teeny place? That's where the camels and oil are?"

"That's it."

Suddenly she clicks off the TV. "Let's eat," she says, and scoops Andrew up for dinner. He squawks in protest, trying to cling to the phone cord, and kicks his little bare feet.

"Come on, buster," she says.

"Where's Jake?" I ask.

Andrew's dad works until six at the smelly paper factory. He's usually here by eight so he can play with Andrew. I figured tonight, because we're eating late, he'd actually have dinner with us for once.

Andrew is howling and making grabbing motions for the phone cord. Mom was pretty mean, scooping him up like that while he was busy.

"I don't know." Mom's voice sounds muddled and shadowy, coming from the kitchen. "Jas, can you clean that up for me?"

Personally, I think Jake should clean off the cord. Andrew's his kid, right? But by the time I get out the sponge and spray cleaner, I decide that thought's unfair. Whose kid is whose. Andrew and I are brother and sister, and that's that.

Jake's probably "out with the guys," which means stopping for a beer on the way home. And one beer means two. But to be fair, usually that's it. He doesn't get drunk. He just likes to socialize. Still, his going out with the guys is one reason Mom won't marry him. They fight about it sometimes.

Dinner is leftover spaghetti warmed in the microwave. But it's delicious. My mom is a great cook. And right after we eat, Andrew has to go to bed. Mom hasn't said another word about camels or Kuwait.

I see headlights. A car is turning off Main Street and coming down the road. Has to be Jake. I can hear the rattle of his VW Golf's loose tailpipe.

The car door bangs. I lean out the back door and wave hi. Jake is thin as a pole. He almost always wears the same clothes—blue jeans and plaid shirt, tucked in. He has a droopy, fox-brown mustache that drives me nuts. An old guy trying to be cool. He's got to be thirty.

"Hey, Jas. How'd it go tonight?"

So he didn't forget my tryout. He just didn't come. Didn't make it.

"Okay," I say, nice and short.

"Yeah? Did you make the team?"

"Yeah." I don't tell him that everybody did.

"My man," he says.

As he comes nearer, I can smell the leftover cigarette and alcohol smell. I am not "his man." He slaps me a high five and I slap back to be polite.

"Mom's putting Andrew to bed. He might be asleep by now," I say quickly. I want him to hear it first from me, to know in advance. He can yell at me, not her.

Jake looks like he's carrying a load of overdue library books, and he can't handle the fine. "What for?"

I shrug. "It's late, I guess. For a baby."

"How am I going to see my son if he's asleep?"

That's not my problem. I want to say to him, Stop by earlier. Andrew's the baby, not you. Come to my tryout. And what I really want to say is, Okay, Andrew's your kid. But what about me? Will I ever be your daughter? Have you ever once thought about that?

He bangs the door closed and brings his smoky smell inside, calling out, "Paula?"

I'm glad Mom hasn't married him. I'm glad her feet are cold.

Now they're arguing about it in a kind of halfhearted way. We're standing in the kitchen.

"I told you not to put him down until I get here. I'll do it, Paula. I'll put him to bed."

"Jake, it's nine o'clock, for heaven's sake. I work all day, do the meals, the laundry. I'm tired, and Andrew's tired. If you want to see him, change your priorities a little. What's so hard about that?"

He opens the refrigerator and pulls out a plate of spaghetti and salad. He takes a piece of garlicky Italian bread that was great-tasting while it was hot. He knocks the refrigerator door closed with his butt, and all the bottles in the door rattle.

But Mom's not paying any attention. She's back in front of the news channel. She turns up the volume. Jake takes his plate and sits beside her. A close-up of an announcer. World news.

*At this hour, we can confirm that the fourth-largest army in the world has just completed its invasion of the tiny country called Kuwait, located at the northern tip of the Persian Gulf. President Bush has responded with a stern warning to the Iraqi dictator, Saddam Hussein, that this type of naked aggression will not be tolerated.*

"Whoa! What's this?" Jake asks. "Who invaded who?"

"Iraq invaded Kuwait."

"Yeah, well, so what? That's a long way from here, isn't it?"

"Oil, Jake. A big piece of the world's oil. Right there. The richest oil reserves in the world. His next move would be Saudi Arabia."

"What's 'naked aggression'?" I ask.

"Naked aggression." Jake laughs. "Good question. I like that. Naked aggression. Could be a name for a rock group, don't you think?" He pops the top to a beer.

But Mom doesn't hear him. From his crib, Andrew lets out a holler. I know he's standing up, clinging to the top railing, feeling left out.

"Can you get him, Jas?" Mom says. Her eyes never leave the screen.

I don't want to. Jake should get him. But now they're talking together in those low voices and mysterious half-sentences grown-ups use when they don't want you to figure out what they're saying. By now I know Iraq is the problem. Saddam and his tanks and now our army, this is what's bothering my mother and all the other grown-ups.

"Yeah. But no one's called you. Get real, Paula."

"But on the five o'clock news I heard this army general talking about an immediate all-out response. A four-star general, General Schwarzkopf, and he has a special plan to deal with Iraq."

I can hear sobs hidden behind her voice. The sound freezes me to the core. She never acts like this. Never.

I go into Andrew's room. The whole room smells of that soft, little, spicy baby smell he has on the top of his head. And it smells of baby powder. His teddy bear night-light glows. There he is, clinging to the railing, in his cotton snap-up pj's, spiky reddish-brown hair every which way. Jake's hair.

"Andrew," I say. "Pumpkin man."

"Ja-ja."

He reaches out his arms.

"Okay, here we go. But you gotta go over the top because I can't work the railing right, all right?"

He's willing. Anything to get out of the crib. I hoist him up and over the railing, bumping his knees a little, but he doesn't complain. Then I settle him on my hip and go to the refrigerator for a four-ounce bottle of apple juice. I take him to the living room.

Jake and Mom aren't talking now. They're staring at a bunch of army guys with pointers and maps. I'm feeling pretty spooked. "Do we have to watch this?"

"Yes." They both speak at once.

Fine. They can, but I'm not. I hand Andrew to Jake, go to my bedroom, and close the door partway. I'm hunting under my pillow for my pajamas when the phone rings. What did Jake mean when he said no one had called Mom?

I hear my mom pick up the receiver. And then I do something I've never done before. The whole day has been so weird. I have to know why. I quietly pick up the receiver by my bed, and, with my hand over the speaker, I listen in.

"Sergeant Paula Williams? This is Captain Orville down at Fort Devens, Massachusetts. This call is to formally notify you that as of tonight at twenty-one hundred hours you are on active deployment. As an equipment and supply battalion officer, you may be one of the first to go to Saudi in advance of the ground troops."

Mom doesn't answer.

"Sergeant Williams?" the captain asks.

"Deployment to Saudi? Is this just a precaution, sir?"

"We want you on our advance supply mission, to arrive in Saudi ahead of the troops. Be ready for mobilization at oh six thirty Saturday morning."

"On Saturday? Wait a minute. Captain, please! I can't go anywhere right now. I know it's the wrong thing to say, but I can't go overseas. I'm a single parent with two children. One's a ten-month-old baby."

"Family arrangements are not the concern of the armed forces. You knew that when you enlisted."

"Yes, sir. But—"

"A refusal to serve means you face a $10,000 fine plus a dishonorable discharge. Your orders are to remain on alert."

"Yes, sir, but could you reconsider? I mean, is there someone I could talk to . . . ?"

The officer has already hung up. My mom is talking to nobody.

I lay down the receiver so, so gently that no one could possibly hear my sneaky *click*. Then I lie on my bed for a minute. I can't think.

I look along the length of my chest. As I breathe, my ribs rise and fall like a boat bottom rocking over waves. And the ocean roars in my ears.

I have just found out my mother might have to do whatever some army captain tells her. I mean, I sort of knew the army was like that. But whenever I visit her at her office, I usually hang around the gumball machine in the lobby or stare at the big wooden eagle hanging on the wall, clutching arrows in his claws, and read the posters about how the army helps you pay for college. I never once thought about the real army, being in a place with bombs and weapons. I don't want any part of this, this officer, this war that just happens one day when you turn on your TV set.

Will she really leave us, me and Andrew, just because that captain guy said so? How can Andrew ever, ever understand this? How can I?

And on Saturday? Leave on Saturday! I can't believe it. I won't believe it.

If I squeeze my eyes tight, then I can freeze everything and make it stand still. I can make the phone call go away if I want.

But . . . but no, I can't. I open my eyes and sit up. Outside my window, night cascades down the tree trunks, spilling into the grass. I march out of my room and down the hall.

# 4

I have to act casual. I want Mom to tell me herself about the call. I don't want her to know I listened in.

I can hear Mom crying. I feel panicky. Saturday is the day after tomorrow. What do they want her to do, go to the desert? How do you live in a desert? I thought deserts were boiling hot and had no water to drink. Maybe this is all nothing. Maybe she'll be gone for only a week. Bring the regular army guys their supplies, set up some tents and food boxes, and then come home. That's not so bad.

"Hey, it's okay, Paula. It's okay," Jake is saying.

I decide it's time for my flashlight walk. When I come back in, I bet she'll be a lot calmer. She's tough. She'll stop crying in a minute.

I hurry through the living room. Jake is holding her in his arms, stroking her head. A minute ago they were arguing about Andrew, now they're acting like lovers. They don't even see me go by.

I get the flashlight from the drawer by the sink and test the battery. Still working. I lay my hand over the top and look at the thin red glow of my blood showing through. Why is our skin so very, very thin? Why isn't our skin harder, stronger, like tree bark maybe, or a clamshell, so we could be safer? Wouldn't that make a ton of sense?

I shiver as I cross the yard, feeling the cool dew bouncing off the stiff grass that brushes against my bare feet. I shine the flashlight up and down my sunflowers. The stalks are bigger than broom handles and furry with a spiky green fuzz. The flowers have been out for nearly two weeks. All day they're covered with crawling bees.

Out by the shed, I'm growing pumpkins for the county fair in September. We got a big load of cow manure from the Parnells, the apple-faced people next door. His brother still keeps some cows, a small herd of Jerseys the color of deer. Cow manure is the key to big pumpkins.

I go around to the side of the shed. The pumpkin vines are still alive, grabbing everything, pulling their way through the grass, across the yard. I squat down and poke the flashlight under some of the big leaves where the pumpkins hide. I hope some will make it until fair time.

With the flat circle of light, I catch the flicker of bat wings in the darkness. Then I bring the flashlight along the grass back to my bare feet, standing side by side in the prickly wet grass. They're long, pale, and narrow, with knobby anklebones. I'm very interested in my feet. At ten months, Andrew's are short and stubby. He can't even stand up on them yet. They look like two lumps of Silly Putty.

Time to go in.

The lights are glaringly bright in the living room. I flop into an armchair. "Hey, Mom, who was that on the phone?"

The TV is off. Andrew has gone back to chewing the phone cord. Jake and Mom are sitting very still on the sofa. Mom's holding a Kleenex, pulling at it, stretching it like it's pizza dough. But it isn't and it rips, it shreds, leaving big holes. Jake still has his arm around her.

"We're going to find a way around this," he says. "Don't worry, all right?"

"Mom?" I have to ask as though I don't know. "Who was on the phone?"

"Nobody. Nobody you know."

"What's going on, then?"

She lifts her head up; her face is wet with tears. My stomach flops. I feel fear tingle up my back from the base of my spine.

"Jake, honey, would you put Andrew to bed? Come here, Jas."

Mom kisses Andrew and Jake carries him, wailing, to his room. I sit beside Mom. When she doesn't say anything, I finally ask, "What?"

She turns to me. "That phone call was from one of my supervisors at Fort Devens. You know I'm in the army reserves, right?"

I nod.

"Well, we have a volunteer army right now. During the Vietnam War, we had a draft, meaning people were chosen to go into the army whether they wanted to or not."

"But that's not fair."

"A lot of people agreed with you. So now, for many reasons, but mostly to save millions of dollars, we have a volunteer army with lots of people like me, who are on reserve."

"Except all you have to do besides go to your office every day is go to Massachusetts sometimes for training."

"Normally, yes. But there is always a small outside chance that the reserves can be called for mobilization. That means called into readiness to help out, called into action."

"You never told me that before."

"To be honest, Jas, I never thought this would happen, my being called to go overseas like this."

"So that phone call, that officer, told you you had to go in the regular army now?"

She nods. "Right."

"And go overseas?"

"Yes, but that's all I know right now. I'll find out more in the morning. Just go to bed, Jas. And don't worry. We'll work something out. See you in the morning."

I go to my room. I plug in my seashell night-light and climb into bed, shoving my toes way down into the cool sheets. I smooth a place on my pillow for my cheek and try to get settled. I tell myself little stories at night when I can't get to sleep. But tonight I can't think of one, and I lie awake for what feels like hours.

# 5

Mom is shaking me. Why? I wonder in my sleep.

"Come on, Jas. Come on, sweetie. Get up."

I hunch up in a ball. Why should I get up? I'm dreaming.

"Sweetie's tired," I say. "Sweetie needs to sleep in."

"Tough. Come on. I have to get a very early start today."

In the hall, Andrew tries to stand up. He trips on the rug and falls down on his little rump. Mom scoops him up. I sit up and push off the crumpled sheet.

"Are you working today?" She's wearing her camouflage uniform.

"I have to go to my office to get some more information."

"What information?"

She shakes her head. "About last night. I'm dropping Andrew off at day care, going in to my office, and I'll be back here to talk with you in about an hour. Okay?"

I nod. She ruffles my hair, and I clench my teeth and let her.

"Where's Jake?" I ask.

"Asleep."

That lazy lummox. My fifth-grade teacher used to say that. Lazy lummox.

"Oh, can you throw in the laundry and take care of those dishes?"

"Yeah. Maybe."

"And take out the trash. To the curb, I mean."

"Yeah."

"And sort the recyclable stuff."

"Okay!"

"Last night I made a couple of lists of phone numbers and a schedule for things like Andrew's one-year checkup—"

"You what?" I stare at her in disbelief. She hugs me.

"Nothing. Forget it. I'm sorry, Jas. I'll be back soon."

Mom puts on dark glasses and gets into her car. I hope it stalls. I hope she is trapped and can't go anywhere. For once, it starts immediately, and she and Andrew back out of the driveway. Mom waves as they pull away.

I watch our ugly car drive up to the stop sign on Main Street. I'll never be like her when I grow up. I will never, ever join the army. I will never, ever leave my children. Ever!

"Ever!" I shout, brushing a few angry tears from my eyes and kicking all the empty plastic milk jugs down the basement stairs, one at a time, happy when they smack against the wall. I hope they wake up Jake.

After eating my cereal, I do the chores, one after another, hardly knowing what I'm doing. I guess her plan is to keep me busy. It works, because soon an hour is up and there she is. She sits me down at the kitchen table. And before she says one word, I feel my whole heart, my whole life, squeeze up in my chest into a terrible, terrible knot.

Say something to make this lump go away, I want to tell her. Then I notice that she looks worse than I do. She's got smoky dark rings under her eyes, and her hair is a disaster.

She can't talk. She holds her car keys and sits with her legs close together and her elbows pulled in tight. She says nothing.

"So?" I say.

"The plan is for me to go with a small advance team. To Saudi Arabia. I'll be setting up, ordering equipment and supplies for a large-scale rapid deployment. The first troops from Fort Bragg will be leaving the U.S. on August 8. That's rapid, all right. Anyway, my first thought was for you kids to go to Grammy and Gramps. But there's no way you can go to Florida. Gramps isn't well at all. Their apartment is so tiny . . . It's better to stay here, at home—so Andrew can go to the same day care, you can stay in the same school."

"Florida? You wanted to send us to Grammy and Gramps? To their one-bedroom apartment with all the medical stuff crammed into it? You were going to send us there?" I can barely breathe.

"No. No, sweetie. It was just a thought . . . I tried contacting your dad to let him know— Anyway it's better, I think, for you both to stay here."

"But who will take care of us?"

"Jake."

"No way!"

"I'm going to leave you the pediatrician's phone number. I've already called her and told her what's going on. And I've asked the Parnells to keep an eye on things."

"The Parnells? Are you crazy?" I shout.

I can't believe this is happening. Mothers don't leave their kids. They just don't. I am no longer angry. I am furious. I miss most of what she is saying.

". . . back I hope by five. There's a homemade pizza in the refrigerator. Cut it in pieces and heat it in the microwave. And there's a tubful of sliced-up carrots and applesauce for Andrew."

"When did you make pizza?"

"Around two in the morning. I had a lot to do."

"But, Mom, I mean, Jake can't . . . he's never even taken care of Andrew. He's late all the time!"

Maybe this is illegal. How can the government take my mother away? I want someone to stop her from going.

"Let's not think about that now, okay? There's still a chance someone will let me stay because of Andrew. Listen, Jas, I'm going back to the office. I have to. I'll be home before five. See if you can go over to Danielle's. And no swimming down at the cove."

"Mom, the water's freezing!"

"See you. Gotta go." She's at the door.

"Mom! No!" I yell. Panic is choking me. "You can't go. Quit! Quit the army, or I'll hate you forever and ever, I swear to God."

Jake comes in, toweling off his hair from the shower. "Hey, hey, let's calm down in here. Give your mom a break, Jas. You think this is easy for her? Stop that yelling."

I turn on him, sobbing. "You . . . you . . . shut up! This isn't even your house."

"Well, I'm sorry, Jas," Jake says, "but it looks like I'll

be moving in here for a while to help out. So you better get used to it."

"Yeah? Well you can stay here for Andrew, then, but don't expect me to follow your dumb rules. I can take care of myself!" I yell.

Now Mom is yelling. "Don't be ridiculous. Stop it, Jas. Stop that!"

Jake gives me a fake smile. "Nice tantrum, but I'm not impressed." He grabs a tee shirt and his car keys. "I'm out of here. I'm going to get a newspaper while you ladies fight this out."

Typical Jake, he disappears before anyone else can. Two seconds later, Mom hugs me, kisses the top of my head, and runs out the door. "See you soon."

And I'm the only one left in the house. Tantrum. What a jerk.

With everyone gone, our little house seems big and empty. I can hear the *thunk, thunk, thunk* of something noisy tumbling over in the dryer. Probably Mom washed Andrew's sneakers. Washed sneakers are never the same. One trip through the washing machine and a sneaker is changed forever. It turns stiff and unfriendly. The laces get weird.

I don't want to be here when Jake gets back with his newspaper. So I call Danielle's house. She's sleeping in. Her mom will have her call me a little later. I go back to the living room and flick on the TV to that cable news station. Sure enough, there's the map. The same one. Someone from the White House is talking.

*This type of aggression will not stand. Right now, we have aircraft carriers in the Persian Gulf. We have fighter aircraft. And we are not alone. The Egyptians and the Saudis are right there with us. Together, with our allies, we will show Saddam Hussein that he cannot invade a defenseless country like Kuwait and get away with it. With our new technology, our new weaponry, Saddam will never know what hit him. Bullies must be punished.*

How can this huge, strange thing be happening to me? Who is this general with the double chin and tiny hat? General Schwarzkopf? Stormin' Norman? Never heard of him till yesterday and now he's ruining my life. I click the TV off fast.

Fighter aircraft. Tomcats. F-16s. I know a little about that stuff from having an air force parent. Mom said that my dad's jet, the Tomcat, can fly eight miles high at the edge of the atmosphere, almost in outer space. He took my mom up in it once, against orders. She said it was like riding in a roller coaster, it was so rattly and noisy. You're in a glass bubble cockpit, and you're spinning around above the earth. And the G forces warp your eyes and face.

The Tomcat is an interceptor. It's supposed to catch

enemy planes and lock on to them with radar and then blow them up before they get near their targets.

But there are other kinds of jets, too. And spy planes, radar jammers, refuelers, missile carriers. And Apache helicopters. All kinds for different jobs. I don't want to think about this. Any of it. So I tie my sneakers and run outside. I usually go down to the beach when I'm upset or want to be alone.

Today it's hot out and a little hazy. The soft, sweet smell of the pink beach roses that grow along the cement steps means there's a little bit of a breeze lifting off the water. I run past the Parnells' house. Muffy is tied up in the backyard, and she yaps at me with her squeaky little bark. "Yap. Yap, yap, yap!"

"Shut up!" I yell back. "Shut up!"

I don't care who hears me. I can't yell at anybody else, so Muffy's going to be the one. Wrong place at the wrong time, as they say on the crime shows.

Across from the Parnells, on the other side of the street, live a man and wife, no kids. The O'Neills. They're lawyers and work late and aren't home a lot. Sometimes I have to walk their dog, Alfonse, an ancient golden retriever with arthritis in his back legs. Alfonse hears Muffy barking and me yelling, and he stands up, tail wagging. Oh no. Maybe he thinks I'm going to walk him, the poor guy.

I run past Alfonse and head down the forty-eight steps to the beach. Most of the rocks here are huge boulders covered with shaggy wet seaweed hair, hanging at low tide like dreadlocks. At low tide, there's sand, some anyway. At high tide, the beach is narrow and rocky. Most of the seaweedy rocks are covered up. Sometimes kids go swimming. Not for very long, though. The water's freezing cold. The warmest it gets is maybe sixty-two degrees, which is cold enough to make my ankles ache in ten seconds.

It's low tide, or almost, and I stumble, trip, and rattle across the rocks to the narrow sandy part. I pick up a big rock and approach the water. I put the rock on my shoulder and heave it. It makes a big, ka-klunking splash with a hollow sound to it. Again and again, I heave another rock, as hard as I can. I'm out of breath now, and I'm crying a little, but I won't stop. I just keep throwing and throwing until I can't anymore. She can't do this to me. Us.

I drop to the sand and roll over onto my stomach. This isn't much of a beach for finding seashells, but there are a few small white cone-shaped twirly ones. The inside curve of seashells reminds me of the soft shape of ears. I sit up and throw a little shell, hard, into the sea.

# 6

At the top of the steps, I see Shawn and Jake coming down the street.

"Shawn!" I yell.

"Jas."

"Hi!" I try to sound a little more cheerful. The first yell came out like a croak. I clear my throat and try again. "Hi!"

Jake must have brought Shawn to look for me. Shawn rolls his eyes at me from behind Jake's back. I smile. Laughter is rising up inside me like a gigantic bubble about to pop.

I squint my eyes against the sun's white glare. The early morning breeze has died down. It won't be until about three o'clock that the onshore breeze starts up and cools things off.

I'm sweaty and my hair is sticking to my forehead. I hate my shirt. Why on earth did Shawn have to show up right now? A half hour later would have been a whole lot better.

Jake seems to be in an awful hurry. He has to be at work by ten.

"Hey, listen, Jas. You better behave yourself today, you got that? No more tantrums. Don't you dare give your mother a hard time when she gets back tonight. Can you imagine what she's going through?"

He turns around and heads back up the street.

I want to say something sarcastic, but manage to keep quiet. I glance at Shawn and make a face.

"Wow," says Shawn. "Is he stressed out or what?"

"Yeah."

"That's your mother's boyfriend, right? What's going on?"

I shake my head, tears rush to my eyes. As I look uphill against the brightness of the sky, Shawn's a blur of white.

"Is it something really bad?" he asks.

"Yeah," I whisper.

"Can you tell me?"

"Yeah, in a minute. Come on."

To make up for not untying Alfonse earlier, I go sit with him in the O'Neills' driveway and scratch him behind his ears. He loves that. Shawn sits near me, watching us. After a few minutes, Alfonse goes over to him and sniffs Shawn's bare arm, then his T-shirt. I brush away my tears.

"Isn't he a great dog?" I ask.

"Yeah. He's cool."

"His name's Alfonse. I visit him a lot because the people who live here are hardly ever home."

"I thought you were going to tell me what's up," Shawn says.

"Yeah. My mom, she got called for mobilization to Saudi Arabia. For the army."

"Whoa. You're kidding."

I shake my head. "I wish I was. She's leaving on Saturday. Tomorrow. And Jake's going to take care of us."

"Wow. That's terrible, Jas. Aren't you scared?"

"Yeah. You think there's going to be a lot of shooting and dropping bombs and stuff?"

"I don't know."

I rest my head on Alfonse. He licks my cheek. I guess he doesn't like to see me cry.

"You were great at the tryouts last night," Shawn says, patting Alfonse, smoothing the hair back on his head. He's looking at Alfonse, not me, when he says this. "It's not every day you get to see Bigfoot try out for basketball."

"Oh. Thanks. But I mean, why did you come? Out of total boredom?"

Instantly I regret what I said.

Shawn looks away and doesn't answer. He takes Alfonse's paws and lays them on his chest. Alfonse thumps his orange tail.

"Hey, Shawn, how about if you don't call me Bigfoot anymore?"

"Yeah. I'll try. But it's asking a lot." He lowers his

head. "Do you miss your family, Alfonse?" he asks in a goofy voice. "Where's your mommy and daddy? Huh? Did they go off and leave you?"

I feel bad that I put Shawn on the spot. I want to make it up to him. I want to make him smile. But the only time I can remember jokes is when I'm lying in bed, trying to fall asleep.

"So . . . ummm . . . what have you been up to all summer?"

"Not much. I've got two ox yearlings that I've been raising, which you probably already know, getting ready for the fall fairs. I was helping my dad some, doing a lot of haying. Went swimming. Went to Eric's house a lot. Hey, Jas, want to come out to my house and meet my oxen sometime?"

"Meet oxen? They're not exactly pets, are they?"

"They're better than pets. They're awesome. A lot of people are telling me they might win best in New England. So, do you want to?" He glances at me hopefully.

"Nah. I don't think so."

Shawn nods and puts Alfonse's paws back down. He gets to his feet and brushes off the seat of his jeans.

I feel rotten. Here he came to my tryout and rode his bike five miles to visit me, and I was mean to him. Twice. I don't know why. I guess he caught me at a bad time.

"I better go," he says. "See ya."

"Yeah." I nod. "See ya." I get to my feet. I have a big lump in my throat, and I let my hair hide my face so he won't see I'm about to cry again.

He heads off alone up the street to get his bike at my house. Then he stops and turns around.

"Oh, wait." He pulls a turquoise envelope out of his jeans. "I meant to give you this."

I take it. "A card? Thanks, Shawn."

He nods and leaves. I open the envelope. Two cartoony cows are standing upright, holding hooves. Inside it says, "I find you udderly delightful!" It's signed "Love, Shawn."

The word "love"—he wrote that! I stare closely at his handwriting. No scribbles, no cross-outs, it's not even teeny writing. He wrote "love" in a normal, confident way.

I kneel there a little longer, hugging Alfonse. I really like the card. What's wrong with me? I guess I'm surprised that Shawn likes me, even though kids were saying it all last year. Still, why was I so mean? All I can think of is that I wanted to hurt him because I'm upset about Mom.

When I get back to the house, I find a mess in the kitchen—Jake's mess: newspapers spread out on the table and a half-empty bowl of Froot Loops. Jake better learn to clean up after himself, I think, because I sure don't want to do it.

I hope Danielle's awake by now. Even if she isn't, I'm going to head on over and sit on her front steps until she is, just to be near some normal folks.

But Danielle is up.

"I have to tell you something important. I'll be right over, okay?"

"Okay, but Stevie's here. The noise level is deafening."

I run through the kitchen and out the back door. I leap onto my bike, no safety helmet, liking how the hot wind blows my hair back away from my face. I ride like a madwoman down Prince Street.

At the Roberges', I push Danielle into her bedroom and shut the door.

"What's the hurry? Hold on while I make my bed," she says.

Danielle is such a neatnik. She wears outfits. Stuff that matches. She even has an "Alcatraz" hat to match the tank top that I borrowed.

"Don't do that now," I say. "Stop, okay? I have to tell you something good and something terrible."

"Well, you can tell me better with the sheets pulled up."

"No, I can't. Danielle, listen. Here's the good part. Shawn came by this morning. And last night he was at our tryouts."

"Really? He must like you. I was right! I told you so, remember? Okay, the sheets will stay messy if it makes you happy."

Danielle picks up her hairbrush and looks in the mirror. She tries to brush her wildly curly hair into shape. She opens her sock drawer and takes out dark purple nail polish, which she hides from Stevie. I snatch it from her, put it back in the drawer, and close it. She thinks this is a normal day, but it isn't.

"No nail polish. Now I have to tell you something truly terrible. Have you been watching the news?"

"The news? No way. What for?"

"Okay. There's this tiny little country called Kuwait. It's like a desert, only underground, under the sand, there's oil—oil for gasoline."

"Oh. Cars." She nods.

Her dad sells hardware and auto parts. Ken's Hardware and Handy. Route 1. Danielle works there on Sundays. I wish I could work there, too. She gets to measure out the nails on a scale and cut lengths of chain and weigh birdseed and everything. I love shoving my arms deep into the huge bags of birdseed. Danielle likes to bop around the store and talk to customers. She can sell them anything. People come in looking for U bolts and walk out with a pack of morning glory seeds and a doggie dish.

"Anyway, there's a war there. Iraq invaded Kuwait and won't leave."

"A war? You're kidding. The United States is at war?"

"No. Not us. Kuwait. It's this place near Saudi Arabia. Last night my mom got called to go by the army, and she went to work this morning to tell them she wants to stay home. But I heard her boss talking. I picked up the phone last night and listened in . . ."

"You did? Did you get caught?"

"No. But this guy, her boss, said family problems were not the army's concern, or something like that. He used a lot of weird words."

"What?" Now Danielle's listening hard. She stares at me, I guess thinking, trying to figure this out. The news is starting to sink in.

"Wait a second. Your mom would leave for war? You mean now? Your grandfather is sick, right? Who's going to stay with you guys?"

"Mom says Jake will."

"This is so, so terrible."

"Yeah, I know," I whisper.

Again I feel a lump in my throat. Tears sting my eyes. I try hard to blink them away. I hate crying. My nose turns big and red and swollen like a clown's, and my eyes turn into puffy slits. I sniff back my tears. "When the going gets tough . . ." The phrase pops into my mind.

"Maybe it will only be for a few weeks. But my mom won't tell me anything."

"If it's only a couple of weeks, you can stay with us. Of course you can. My mother won't mind."

"I don't think so, Danielle. Maybe I could, but what about Andrew? Where would he go? What about Stevie? Your mom's already worn out. She's about ready to pop a gusset as it is."

"Yeah. But I know she'd let you. And somebody else could take Andrew . . ."

"No! Nobody's going to split us up!" I shout. "Okay?"

"Okay, Jas. Jeez, I'm sorry. I was just trying to think this through. Wait. Come on down to the basement. We can check the war thing out. Maybe you've got it all wrong."

I feel better already. I know I can always count on Danielle.

In the family room, Danielle turns on the set, and we flop onto an old sofa to watch.

"Flip to the news channel," I say. "It's on all the time. You'd think this desert stuff was World War III or something." I laugh nervously.

Danielle glances at me, then at the map, now in a little corner of the screen.

*Despite warnings from the United States and the world community, Saddam Hussein continues his policy of belligerence and aggression. He has taken hundreds of hostages, British, American, and other nationalities, and is holding them in the American embassy in Kuwait, while he waits for the United States to stop its so-called aggression against the Arab peoples.*

A videotape of Saddam Hussein appears on the screen. He's sitting in a big armchair, wearing army clothes and a beret, and he has a thick black mustache that looks glued on. An Iraqi flag is placed next to his chair, and standing on either side of him is a line of British hostages.

Saddam is smiling broadly. He reaches out his hand, and suddenly a little boy is pushed forward by the soldiers in the background. The boy has his hands clasped in front of him. He is wearing a white shirt and pale blue shorts. His hair is blond and very neatly combed. He stares to the side at a big plant. He won't look straight ahead.

The television voice says, "This is Stuart, a five-year-old British subject in captivity. Saddam is ordering the boy to tell the cameras how well he is being cared for as a guest. They are giving him Corn Flakes, his favorite food."

Danielle gasps. "Oh my God, what's happening to him? He looks terrified."

I'm clenching my hands so tightly that my fingernails are digging into my palms. "He's a hostage." What if Mom goes there and gets taken hostage? I never even thought of that last night. Where's Stuart's mother? Only soldiers and Saddam are near him.

Saddam tries to turn the boy to face the cameras more directly. Stuart won't budge. He stiffens his little body. And if Saddam tries to force him in front of international television, it will be clear, even more clear, that something is terribly, terribly wrong. I feel a flash of pride that one little boy could be so brave.

Again the news station flashes a statement from President Bush.

*The capture and holding of civilians is a clear viola-*
*tion of international law. It will be met with as much*
*force as necessary, even lethal force, if diplomacy fails.*

"Lethal force?" Danielle asks.

"He means our army can kill those soldiers. Here. Turn it off." I grab the remote and click it.

"That poor little kid. Do you think the Iraqi soldiers will kill him?" Danielle asks in a small voice.

"I don't know." Neither one of us knows what to say.

"We should go out and start practicing layups before it gets too hot," Danielle finally says, always practical.

"It's already too hot."

"Well, then what do you want to do?"

"I don't know. I have no clue."

"At noon, I have to go volunteer at the stables. Want to come?"

"Yeah. Sure. With Stevie, right?"

"Yeah."

Part of Stevie's summer program is lessons at a thera-peutic riding program. The lessons are expensive, so Danielle's whole family pitches in alongside Stevie to do work around the stables. I've been along a couple of times. It's fun.

"You really think working with the horses is helping him?"

"I don't know. A little. He does great while he's there, but then when he comes home, he's the same. Yelling and screaming, doing whatever he feels like."

"But he's good there because he knows the horses won't like it if he's noisy?"

"Yeah," says Danielle. "He likes the horses better than us, I swear to God. He finds them calming."

"Well, animals are sort of better than people."

Upstairs we can hear a high-pitched shriek and the sound of Stevie's running feet.

"Stevie, we're leaving for the stable now!" Danielle's mother speaks loudly and firmly. "No food. Put the crackers back."

Stevie gives a stiff laugh and runs into his bedroom. Danielle and I go upstairs and head for the car so he won't have an audience other than his mother.

Soon Mrs. Roberge comes out to join us girls. Danielle's mother is short and has curly brown hair. Her favorite color is red. Today she's wearing red pants and a red T-shirt, with red sandals and red toenail polish. Not exactly camouflage colors.

"Whoof! It's hot and muggy," she says as she opens the car door to air out the interior. They have a brand-new Honda and it has New Car Smell. She turns on the engine and starts the air conditioning full blast. Mainers don't like to be too warm even for a few minutes. "Jas, you were great last night, I hear."

"Mom," Danielle says, "you won't believe what happened. You know how Jas's mom is in the army reserves? Well, last night she got called up!"

"To go to Saudi Arabia? My gosh!" Mrs. Roberge stares at me. "When will she have to leave, Jasmyn?"

49

"Saturday morning."

"You mean tomorrow?"

I nod. "She's going to be among the first to go."

"My God. She must be going out of her mind. What's she going to do?"

"She has to go. You can't say no to the army. And I guess Jake will take care of me and Andrew."

"Well, you tell your mother that anytime I can I'll—"

At that moment Stevie blasts through the front door and Mrs. Roberge is sucked back into watching out for him, getting him into the car, buckling his seat belt—all those details—and she never gets to finish what she was saying.

After Stevie's lesson, as we pull back into the Roberges' driveway, Danielle shouts, "Phone! The phone's ringing! I'll get it!" She dashes into the house.

She leans out the front door. "It's Bridget and Amy. They're going to meet us at your hoop so we can practice for today, okay?"

No. It's not okay. But I nod. I can't handle even the thought of dealing with Bridget today. I just don't have the energy.

The four of us play for nearly three quarters of an hour. Muffy barks nonstop. Because of our height, it's me vs. Bridget as forwards, and Danielle vs. Amy as guards. So I have to shoot past Bridget. And today I can't jump. I feel nailed to the ground.

Every time Bridget scores, she sings "Can't Touch

This." Once, she tells us, "The whole time I was at Red Star camp, we sang that. It was so awesome."

She elbows Danielle in the arm, trying to snatch the ball away.

"Foul!" Danielle yells.

"No way!" Bridget snatches the ball now that play has stopped. She dribbles once and shoots.

"It was too a foul. You jammed her with your elbow," I say. "I saw you."

"Amy, did you see me do that?" Bridget asks.

"No."

Finally we all stop, hot and winded, hands on our knees to catch our breath.

"Phew, it's hot. I'm going in for a glass of water," Bridget says.

"Oh, sure. I should have offered."

The rest of us flop down in the grass to wait. But Bridget doesn't come out right away. I figure she's using the bathroom.

Suddenly the back door bursts open. She's got something in her hand. "Look at this!" She's waving my card from Shawn. "Two cows. Can you believe it? Cows. That is so completely country! It's so hick. It says, 'I find you udderly delightful.' And it's signed 'Love, Shawn.' "

Amy shrieks with laughter and runs to the door, yelling, "Let me see. Let me see."

I lay my head on my drawn-up knees and decide to sleep. Danielle snatches the card from Amy and brings it

51

to me. Without even looking, I tear it to shreds, and when I get to my feet, I toss the little pieces of paper down the storm drain.

"It was only a joke, Bridget. He gave it to me as a joke," I say, pulling the elastic band in my ponytail tighter.

"Yeah? I don't know, Jas. We all know how much Shawn loves cows. Doesn't look like a joke to me. Udderly delightful. Come on, Amy. We're going back-to-school shopping later on."

"You are? Where?" Danielle asks, suddenly interested. She and her mom are shop-till-you-drop types. You have to be if you want to wear things that match. "The mall?"

"Yeah. You want to come?"

"Sure," Danielle says. "You want to, Jas?"

I shouldn't, because Mom is leaving tomorrow; I should stay here. And suddenly I hate them. I hate their bikes. I hate their trip to the mall.

I shake my head. "Nah."

"Oh, how udderly too bad," Bridget says, swinging her leg across her bike and pedaling up the street with Amy. "See you later, Jas."

"Wait up!" Danielle is right behind them. "See ya, Jas."

I walk down to the O'Neills' yard to see Alfonse. The hot silence of an early August afternoon settles into my ears. High above the cove, seagulls float in circles.

Crickets chirp in the dry grass. There, where no one can hear me, I burst into tears. How could I go to the mall, when all that's in my head are the words "Don't go, Mom, don't go."

# 7

Later, while I'm pulling the homemade pizza out of the refrigerator and hunting around for the carrots and applesauce, Mom turns in the driveway with Andrew in the back seat.

I run to the window, trying to see if Mom looks happy or sad. Maybe everything's okay.

I burst out the back door and meet them at the car.

"Hi, Mom! What happened?"

Mom gives a tired smile as she lifts Andrew from the back seat. Andrew buries his face in her neck and looks at me sideways. He holds his blanket straight out, giving it to me.

"Oh, thank you, Andrew."

I take it. Now he wants it back. I give it back. Little kids think that's playing, the same way they think throwing their toys out of the crib is hilarious because then you have to pick them up.

"Mom? What happened?" I repeat.

"Well, basically nothing happened. I talked to two different supervising officers. Neither one said anything new. Then I met my replacement and worked with him for a few hours, and that was it."

"They showed a little boy on TV today," I say slowly. "I think he's a hostage maybe."

"Listen. Let's sit down and eat and have a nice supper. We'll watch the news later."

"Okay." I would like it better if we never watched the news again.

We hear the toot of a horn. Jake is making the turn off Main Street. He pulls into the driveway and jumps out of the car. This is amazing. He must have left work early! So he can be on time if he wants to.

"Hey, how'd it go?" He lifts Andrew from her.

"All right, I guess. I mean, I did what I could. The army doesn't tell you anything. I asked how long the assignment would be. They don't answer questions. They listen. So." She shrugs.

"Didn't they tell you how long you'd be gone? Two weeks? Six months?"

"They give out information on a 'need to know' basis only."

"Need to know. I like that. What the heck does that mean?" Jake says angrily. "That's exactly the point. We need to know."

She leans her head against his shoulder.

"Not your need, Jake. Their need, silly. In the army, you follow orders; you don't give them. I bet Jas has dinner ready for us. She's such a good kid."

We go up the back steps and file into the house in a strange silence. Jake gets the window fan from Mom's bedroom because the kitchen is hot, and Mom puts Andrew in his high chair with a plastic bib tied around his neck. She hands him a tiny slice of warm pizza, while she stirs a pitcher of lemonade.

She gives Andrew one of those baby cups of milk with the spout top and two handles. It's got a roly-poly bottom so it won't tip over. He carefully pulls gooey mozzarella cheese off the top of his pizza and puts it in his mouth. The cheese is oily and turns his chin shiny.

The pizza tastes really good, at least the first few bites do, but I'm having a hard time noticing. I don't even know how many slices I've eaten. Then, at one minute before six, the telephone rings.

Jake snatches it. "Yes, hello?"

Without another word, he hands the phone to my mom. She jumps up and stretches the cord out of the kitchen into the living room, so it's hard for us to hear. Jake and I sit frozen in position.

"Yes, sir. I understand that. . . . No. There is no problem. . . . Yes, sir. Six-thirty a.m."

She doesn't come back to the table, so we have to get up. She's standing in the living room, staring out the front window so that she's looking at the Parnells', and beyond their house the tip of Moorhead Island and the flat stripe of blue ocean, holding the phone at her side, down by her thigh, the cord twirled and knotted around her other finger. And she's crying.

Gently Jake takes the receiver from her hand and hangs it up. He makes her sit in the armchair, and he kneels in front of her. "What did he say, Paula?"

"Just confirming my deployment. It's going to be a large-scale mobilization. I'll be in Saudi Arabia by Tuesday. I leave at six-thirty tomorrow morning. I can't do this to my kids. I'm a good soldier. But I can't do this, Jake," she whispers. "I can't. And I have to."

She closes her eyes. She sways as if she's going to faint. My heart is pounding. Is she okay? I stare at her. Suddenly her eyes open again, focusing on Jake.

"You've got to help me, Jake. Please. You've got to come through for me. There's no one else."

"All right, now. All right. We can think this through."

Mom shakes her head. "No. We can't. I thought all day. There's nothing left to think."

"What about like we said last night? I take the baby. I take Andrew, and Jas goes to her real dad's."

"You mean you called to send me there? Japan?" I yell. "No! I don't even know my 'real' dad."

"No. *I* called him," Mom says. "There's no way, Jake."

At that moment I hate Jake. I turn and glare at him, ready to spit and kick and fight. "And you—you— you're not taking my baby brother away from me. Ever!"

And then we're all quiet for a minute, letting things sink in. In a shrunken voice, I ask, "Mommy, are you going to be in a war?"

"No. Of course not. I'm not a combat soldier. I'm in a supply battalion," Mom says. She comes over and leads me to the sofa so we can sit together. "The army needs lots and lots of supplies, and I have to keep track of that."

She hugs me, but I resist. Of course she'll be in a war, I think bitterly. That's what soldiers do. They fight in wars. Why is my mother going? If she loved me and Andrew enough, she wouldn't go. War means she could be killed. And what if she had to kill someone else?

I can't stand it. I run to my room and slam the door. I pull my pillow to my face and sob into it. I hate her. I hate her.

Then, sobbing leftover, bump-in-the-road sobs, I go to my desk and snatch a pencil and writing pad. I will leave home right now.

*Dear Mom,*

*I would never do this to you, I mean leave you. I hope you believe me. I'm going to run away so you can't do this to me again. I will come get Andrew as soon as possible. Don't worry—we'll be fine without you.*

*Love, Jas.*
*Age 11, nearly 12.*
*12th birthday in one month.*

That's good. Twelve seems old. I'm tall enough to pass for fourteen. I bet I'll be able to get a job. I rip the paper off the notepad, accidentally tearing it down the middle. So I have to hunt for the Scotch tape. All patched together, the note doesn't look quite as official. I stomp over to my door and fling it open. There's Mom on the other side, looking startled. I guess she was about to come in.

"Excuse me," I mutter, trying to push past her.

"What's this?" she asks, reaching for the paper. I had thought I'd leave it on the kitchen table for tomorrow morning, so I could get a hefty head start tonight. I was going to hide at the stable and decide what to do from there.

She pulls the note from my fingers and reads it more than once—maybe she's memorizing it.

"Here, sweetie. Come over here." She leads me to my bed with her arm around me. "What's this crazy stuff, huh?"

I'm crying now, but I'm still determined to at least get to my closet and fling a few clothes together. My maroon Pre-season League jersey. I grab it.

"Put the shirt down. Come on, now. How about a back rub?"

Back rubs always calm me down. She knows that. Nobody else does. Slowly and gently Mom pushes all the stiffness from my shoulders and the back of my neck.

Jake comes in and watches. "Maybe we should get

married tonight," Jake says. "That's what a lot of reservists are doing. I heard it on the noon news. So whaddya say? You want to?"

"What?" Mom stares at him.

"I'm serious, Paula. Legally, it might be a good idea, in case . . ." He stops talking for a moment.

"Oh, come on, Jake. That's silly. I'm going to be fine. Anyway, we can't get married tonight. This isn't Hollywood or Las Vegas. I mean, I hardly know what I'm doing."

"I think we should," Jake says. "I love you, Paula. For God's sake."

"Jake, please don't do this right now. I'm not like you. I'm not one person. I'm three people all in one. That's what a mother is."

She shakes her head, her eyes full of tears. "That's what I tried to tell the officers today."

It's not going to work out, this Jake-staying-here-with-us thing. He can't even handle dropping in now and then. He thinks he can sit around with a beer for the whole evening and not do the laundry. He has no idea how hard my mom works. Worse yet, he wanted to send me to Japan.

Later I'm brushing my teeth. I hear them in Mom's bedroom. Andrew's sleeping. I tiptoe to the open door of the bathroom, right next to her room, and listen.

"You don't know, Paula. Listen to me. I work all day long with guys who've been in the army. You should hear them. They're going to harass the daylights out of you over there. And where do you think you're going to go to the bathroom in the desert? Even a little thing like that. You think the guys are going to put up a little curtain around you so you can have some privacy? You don't know how guys think, Paula. I do. This isn't going to be some picnic at the office. It's going to be rough."

"Listen, Jake, I've been through years of training. Ten years. I know these guys, too. I know there'll be a lot of gross comments to deal with. That's not new. I'll be okay. I'll manage. Hey, I lift weights, you know. I'm strong."

She's trying to joke him along.

"Not as strong as a guy. Especially in a war zone. Man, guys freak out under that kind of pressure. There won't be anybody there . . . there won't be me there . . . to protect you, to help you."

I peek around the door. Jake's got his arms around my mom, and he's crying.

"I love you, Paula. Don't forget that. Please?"

I run down the hall to my room and plug in my seashell night-light. We have to get up at five-thirty to take Mom to the bus. It's the first time I've ever seen how much Jake cares about Mom. He's so worried. Maybe more than I am. And that scares me worse than anything.

I lie huddled under a thin cotton blanket. "Don't go, Mommy. Please. I love you," is running over and over in my head, and then suddenly those words switch to angry ones—"How can you leave us?"

When my eyes are closed, I see the white, pencil-shaped, computer-guided missiles being loaded onto planes. Are those some of the supplies Mom is in charge of? Please, God, I hope not.

# 8

At five-thirty, Mom is up. She opens my door. "Come on, sweetheart."

I roll over and sit up. "But, Mom, why do you have to go? Why can't they send someone else?"

Mom sighs. "I've been in the army reserve for ten years, Jas. My unit's been called."

I fling back the sheets.

"Okay?" Mom asks.

I shrug, not willing to answer. "Whatever," I mumble. I pull on my shorts and tee shirt and pull my hair back into a ponytail. My sneakers are in the kitchen by the back door.

I grab a bowl of Cheerios and half a banana and sit

down to eat. Everyone is silent. Already Mom's two backpacks are sitting near the door.

"When did you pack?" I ask.

"Last night."

"Did you say you were leaving from the Greyhound station?" Jake asks.

"Yes. Now, this little notebook is Andrew's immunization record. He has his one-year checkup in October. And Jas will need to go back-to-school shopping at the mall for new sneakers and notebooks and so on . . ."

"Hold it," Jake says. "It's five forty-five in the morning. Slow down."

I shovel in the rest of my Cheerios and rinse my bowl. I start to put the bowl in the sink.

"Dishwasher," Jake says without looking at me.

I turn around with a glare that could cut cold steel.

"Jas, please," says Mom. She's really saying, Let's not get in a fight here. Not now.

"Okay, okay," I grumble. I pull open the dishwasher and put my bowl inside. "I'm waiting at the car."

I push through the back door and head out to my sunflowers. The sun is just coming up over the ocean, a streak of rosy bright pink fading to a vivid pink-orange along the water. I stretch out my arms so the light can slide up them. Tears are just behind my eyes again. The only way I can stop them from coming is to be angry. Angry at everybody—except Andrew. And when I think of Andrew, I'm scared. Really scared. Because when you get right down to it, Jake doesn't know how to take care of a baby, and everybody knows it.

They're coming out of the house. Andrew is wrapped up in his blanket, Binky. Jake has the two backpacks. Mom's wearing dark glasses again. Trying to prove she's tough? I throw myself in the back seat and slam the door.

All the way to the bus station, twenty minutes, I don't say a word.

Mom keeps saying things like, "I'll call you as soon as I land in Europe. Probably from Spain, when we refuel. And then I'll try to call again from Saudi Arabia. You guys can write to me at an APO address. I'll give it to you when I get there. So you won't need to buy air-mail stamps."

Like I'm going to write. She doesn't want to hear what I have to say.

"Well, you're coming back when Stuart gets released, right?" I say finally. "So what's the big deal? How hard can it be to get a little kid released?"

Jake and Mom look at each other.

"You're right," Mom says. "In a few weeks, this could all be over."

"You said by basketball season for sure, remember? Hey, by the way, I start practice on Monday."

Nobody says anything.

"Yoo-hoo. Mom? I have basketball every afternoon next week. Three to five. I'm the team captain, remember? I have to be there."

"Okay, sweetie. You'll get there. Don't worry. Jake'll come home and pick up Andrew. Don't worry about a thing."

"Oh? Jake will, will he?" he says under his breath. "How am I going to manage that, Paula? Cut my work by more than five hours per week, so it fits in with Andrew's day-care hours?"

"Then Jas can get him," Mom says. "That might work. Jas, honey, you can leave practice a little before five, can't you?"

"Well, if it's practice, yeah. But what if it's a Preseason game? What if it's an away game?"

Jake interrupts us. "Listen, Jas, tell the coach you can play, but you can't be captain this summer. There's no way I can guarantee you'll be there. There must be some other girl who can take over for you."

I can play, but not be captain? Of course, Coach would pick Bridget next. I feel a big chunk of my life break off like a piece of ice in a river and swirl away downstream.

"No way!" I yell. "I can't believe you said that."

"Please, let's not argue. I'm sure there's some way to figure this out," Mom says.

Right near the bus station, Jake makes a wrong turn. He swears and hits the steering wheel with his palm. He turns around and glares at me, as though I made him do it.

I glare right back at him. "What?"

Mom lays a hand on his arm.

"It's okay," she says softly.

He shakes his head and puts his hand on her leg. They sit that way, connected, for a minute. His eyes are full of tears. I sit way back in the seat and rest my head against the window. I push hard till my forehead hurts.

Andrew doesn't have a clue. He's rocking in his seat, looking at the cars and trucks, singing a little chant with no words.

Jake parks the car and we get out. The sun is up, but in coastal Maine there is still a morning chill in the air. The bus isn't here yet. Already other families are waiting, standing in silent circles, separate little groups holding one another closely. I don't see anyone else from Stroudwater, which isn't surprising considering how small a town it is.

Everyone tries to give everyone else privacy, but we're right across the street from a Burger King and a doughnut shop, and a lot of people are driving to work at the hospital at the top of the hill, slowing down to stare. I turn my back to them.

I stand rigid as a pencil. Mom's hugging Andrew, and Jake's got his arms around both of them. I could be the planet Pluto as far as they're concerned.

"Hey," Mom says to me. "Come here."

She hands Andrew to Jake and wraps her arms around me, but I don't soften up and hug back. How can I? She can't be doing this to us. She can't.

The bus pulls up and lumbers into its parking lane, swaying from side to side like an old polar bear at the

zoo, the kind with the chlorine-blue fur. The other soldiers start lining up, their families hurrying back to their
cars because they're crying so much. Jake takes Mom's
packs one at a time and tosses them into the luggage
space under the bus.

Mom bends down and pushes up her dark glasses so
she can see me. "I love you, Jas. You have no idea how
much."

Then she kisses Jake and Andrew fastest of all and
hurries to take a place in line. Andrew starts to wail.

"Hush, Andrew," Jake says, jiggling him up and
down. Mom turns and tries to smile at us from the top
step, then disappears. Behind the tinted windows, she is
lost from view.

All the way home, the only thing I can think about is
how mean I was to Mom. I didn't tell her I loved her. I
didn't tell her not to worry. I didn't help with Andrew. I
stood still, still as a little toy soldier. Made of metal,
arms at my sides. Metal, cold and hard. And heartless.

What if Mom dies and never comes back? I didn't say
one nice thing today. I'm not even sure I said goodbye.

Tears begin to run down my face. Andrew rocks in his
car seat.

"Mama?" he says to me. "Mama?"

"No, not now," I tell him. "She's gone."

# 9

"So," says Jake brightly as we pull into the driveway. "This is it. Ta-dah! We're home."

He lifts Andrew out and swings him up in the air. Andrew starts his great big laugh, and even I have to smile a little.

Jake notices. "Life's going to go on, Jas. It has to."

"I just don't understand." I flop against the side of the VW.

"Jas, you have to let her go. She's doing something she believes in. Serving her country. Helping people who need help. She believes in that. She's trained for that for ten years, Jas."

"Well, nobody ever told me," I mutter.

"Nobody told you what?"

"Nobody ever told me that going to her office job in Portland was the same thing as being ready to be part of a real live war in the middle of a stupid desert."

Jake looks at me. "Oh. I see what you mean. Yeah, I can understand that. I can see how you wouldn't make the connection."

In the grass by the driveway, Jake finds a squishy pink ball that used to be mine. I always liked it a lot. He tosses it lightly to Andrew, who is sitting in the grass.

"Here, Andrew. Catch! Whoa, buddy. You missed."

The ball rolls across the driveway. Andrew crawls after it at a hundred miles per hour. He wears the knees smooth on his overalls. They all have iron-on patches inside and out.

"So, Jake, about basketball . . ."

"Not now, Jas. I can't deal with it right now." He holds up both hands like a policeman saying "Stop."

But that's not fair. I can't *not* deal with it!

I give a huge sigh. I have a colossal headache, and I feel groggy from getting up so early. I decide to go down to the cove.

Directly across from me is a small island, Moorhead Island. The O'Neills paddle over there sometimes in their two-man kayak and circle it. I've been wanting to paddle there for years, but you have to cross the shipping channel, and the big tankers can't see kayaks very well.

Two long-necked cormorants, black-feathered and gawky, stand on the rocks, drying their wings. Witch birds.

For some reason, right at that moment I turn around. Jake is standing at the top of the steps, watching me. He's holding Andrew. Another family with little children is slowly descending the cement staircase for a Saturday morning at the beach. I can smell their SP45 sunblock from here.

"What?" I shout.

"Come on," Jake says. "We're going to McDonald's for an early lunch. For a treat."

He has to be kidding. Maybe babies think McDonald's is a treat, but seventh graders sure don't.

I squint up at him. "Nah. That's okay. You go. I'll get something at home."

"Jas! Come on!"

The family stumbles past me with their bright yellow sand pails, clutching towels, tottering on the loose rocks.

"What? I don't want to go, that's all. I'm not hungry."

He shifts Andrew to the other arm. Andrew lunges toward the water and kicks to be put down. I'll go, I guess. I start walking toward the house. But I'm not eating a damn thing.

If Jake gets sick of me, he can't send me to Japan against my will, can he?

Jake's in the kitchen, checking his wallet for money. "Can I talk to you?" he asks.

I flop into a chair, stare at the ceiling. "Yeah."

"We're going to get through this, Jas. I think you're scared by the word 'war.' We both are. But you have to understand that it's not a war at all. I bet it'll be over in a few weeks. Maybe a month."

"A month? So you do think she'll be back after that hostage kid, Stuart, gets released? You think so?"

"Yup. As soon as the hostages are released, the reserve troops will probably be sent home."

"Not in time for my birthday?"

But he's not listening now. He's looking for the keys. And muttering. "Money. Keys. Kid. Come on, Andrew." Andrew is under the table, locating lost Cheerios one by one and eating them.

"You made Mom call my dad in Japan, didn't you? I bet you told her to do it when she went to her office, so I wouldn't hear."

He nods.

"Well, you should never have done that!" I yell. "I'm staying with Andrew. He needs me."

"Hey! Don't yell, all right? Come on, Jas. Look. Can we just go for lunch?" He steps outside with Andrew. "Come on."

I don't move an inch. "You don't want me here, do you?"

"Jas, stop it. You're making it sound really bad, but the . . . uh . . . problem isn't personal. It's just that I don't know how we're going to manage. You and I, I mean," he says. "I never had an eleven-year-old girl before, and I'm just learning about the baby. Maybe Mrs. Roberge can help out in the afternoon or something."

"Are you crazy? Mrs. Roberge? Have you spent an hour with Stevie lately?"

"Jasmyn, look. I don't care. Stay here. Forget McDonald's. We'll be home later. If you're not going to come, you could at least write your mom a letter. We'll get the APO when she calls."

He jogs down the steps, and a moment later heads up the street with Andrew in his VW. Jake has already moved Andrew's car seat into the back of his VW. He hates Mom's big bomb of an Oldsmobile.

I go to my room for a nap. I'm not very good at writing letters. It's far, far easier to sleep.

Sunday is a strangely hollow, flat day. The water in the cove is milky white and still. Andrew is fussy. His gum is swollen and red in the back, where one of his one-year molars is trying to push through. He's always had a hard time teething.

"Think he's sick?" Jake asks for the tenth time.

"He's teething." I show Jake the sore place in Andrew's mouth. "See?"

"Well, what does your mom do? Should I call the doctor?"

"Yeah. If you want. But Mom just gives him baby aspirin and Popsicles to calm him down."

Jake just about tears the bathroom apart looking for the little bottle of baby aspirin. Of course he doesn't find it there because it's in the top drawer of Andrew's dresser in Andrew's bedroom. I have to go find it for him.

I don't have any energy today. I feel so bad for the way I treated Mom at the bus station yesterday that my stomach is in knots, and I have a pounding headache.

I am lying on my stomach in the living room, reading *The Black Stallion* for the millionth time. I'm going to read through the whole *Black Stallion* series again. Whenever I'm upset, I reread books over and over. I like doing it. A lot of kids like doing it. For some reason, teachers hate it.

A little later, Jake comes back into the living room, pulling a sweatshirt over Andrew's head.

"I'm taking Andrew for a walk in his stroller. You want to come?"

"Huh? Oh. No."

He stands there, not satisfied, staring down at me.

"Listen. I want you to write your mother today, since you didn't do it yesterday."

"Are you kidding? She just left! She didn't even get there yet."

I uncoil my sarcasm as though it were a venomous snake, a coiled cobra raising its head. I think both Jake and I know that if there's going to be a fight, I am going to win.

He turns away from me.

"I still think you should write her. Imagine how she feels right now. Can you think of that for two seconds?"

I, the cobra, stay poised, head raised, the whole time he's in the house. When he leaves, I droop, rest my aching head on my arms. I want to write to Mom so badly. But I won't. She has to be punished.

I wait till Jake has left the house. Then I call Shawn.

"Hey, it's me. Jasmyn. I'm sorry about being in a bad mood the other day. I really like the card you gave me."

"Oh, yeah? You do?"

"It's nice."

"So, what are you doing?"

"I'm supposed to write my mom a letter."

"That's a good idea. I bet she misses you already."

"Yeah, but, Shawn, I can't. Want to know what I have down so far?"

"Sure."

" 'Dear Mom'—that's it. And I did that yesterday. Maybe I should send her a postcard."

"No. No way. Mothers don't want that. She wants you. Anything from you. Put the letter under your pillow for a while. Maybe it will smell like you."

"That's ridiculous."

"No, it's not."

"Well, anyway. That's all I'm doing."

"I better go. Eric's over at my house right now."

"Okay. See ya."

All right, Jasmyn, write this letter. The tough get going, right? I'm writing it. Right now. Even if I don't have anything good to say.

*Dear Mom,*

*I am so worried. Jake says it's not a war right now. But why are we sending weapons there? What if you get hurt? Did you think of that? Andrew has been very, very fussy. I think it's his back tooth. Jake took him for a walk.*

*Love,*
*Jas*

I get an envelope, fold the letter, put it inside—but then what? I don't even have an APO yet. My mom is lost somewhere in Spain or the Arabian desert. I don't really know where she is.

# 10

Next morning, Monday, Jake is tapping at my door. He's holding Andrew, whose red cheeks creased with lines from the folds in the sheet mean he just woke up, too. Maybe we can sleep for a few weeks until Mom gets home. It's nine-thirty.

"I gotta get ready for work now, Jas. I'll take Andrew to day care. But you'll have to walk down and pick him up. When does your mom usually get him? Four-thirty? They close by five, right? I get off work at six, but by the time I punch out and drive across town, it's at least six-fifteen."

"Six-fifteen? Mom got home at four-thirty, no matter what. I have basketball practice this afternoon until five. Remember? I told you in the car. I'm team captain."

"You'll have to skip it, Jas. Be reasonable. You can't be

captain this time around. I'm sure your coach will understand. It's not your fault. And what's the point of this summer league anyway? It's August. You should be lying around in a hammock reading comic books or . . . or selling lemonade or picking blueberries. Your first real game isn't till November 15, right? So give me a break."

I try to be patient, but I want to scream. Jake acts so incredibly *old*.

"Maybe you used to read comic books and stuff, but that was the old days. It's not like that now. Basketball is really competitive. Coach Campbell scheduled us for gym time all week. Then we have games. I have to be there. He's counting on me."

"Oh yeah? Well, we're all counting on me, so you'll have to call him and tell him you can't come."

I jump out of bed and follow him into the hall. "I won't do that. I can't do that."

"If you won't call him, then I will."

"No! No."

Jake frowns and turns away, heading toward the kitchen. "I'm going to be late for work. We'll have to talk about this later."

I follow him. He picks up Andrew's diaper bag and slings it over his shoulder. He's not even going to discuss it.

"Jake!" I yell. "Come on! I have to be there."

"Sorry, Jas. You'll have to call him. What am I supposed to do? Leave work so you can go to practice? Think about that for two seconds."

Out in the driveway, he straps Andrew into his car seat.

"Why should I? Why should I think about that? You don't think about me. Ever. You wanted to send me to Japan."

"Yeah. And you know why? This. This is exactly why. How can I possibly take care of both you guys and go to work? My first day doing it, and I'm already screwed. I'm late."

He gets into the VW and slams the door, then pokes his head out the window.

"If I don't work, we don't eat. Right? By the way, I put Andrew's stroller in the shed."

"Hey!" I shout at him. "How were you going to pick up Andrew if you sent me to Japan?"

"I didn't send you, did I?" he says, not answering the question. He gives me a little wave as though nothing's wrong, then drives off with Andrew.

I sink down on the back steps. What am I going to do? We have practice every afternoon this week from three to five. And after that we have six games, two a week. I have to be there, that's all there is to it. Maybe—maybe—it would be all right to leave practice fifteen minutes early to get Andrew. But it would not be okay under any circumstances to leave a game fifteen minutes early, and we have four away games. If I give up being captain, I know Coach will give the job to Bridget. He'll have to.

Back in the kitchen, I fix myself a peanut butter and jelly sandwich. Looks like Jake did the same thing. He didn't clean up at all this morning! The sink is full of dirty dishes now, cereal bowls, spoons, gooey knives. I should rinse them and put them in the dishwasher, but I don't. By dinnertime, the kitchen will be a total mess.

And what are we going to do for dinner tonight? Mom always had dinner lined up in advance, so that when she got home, she just had to warm things up for a few minutes in the microwave. I open the refrigerator, hunting for signs of dinner. Pasta sauce? No. A fish chowder? No. Hamburger patties all ready to go? No. Carrot sticks in a little plastic tub? Nowhere in sight.

Nice going, Jake. I slam the door. It's true that he sent out for Chinese food for the weekend, but he sure isn't prepared for a day when he has to work.

I wander into the living room. The TV sits like a big, dark-screened monster in the corner. A scary black crystal ball full of killings. Real ones, not cartoon ones. I don't want to watch it, but I flick it on anyway and flop onto the sofa. Back to the news channel. I'm addicted. I have to know what's going on.

*American ships are already in the area in a show of force to warn Saddam that the world means business. The army has called this marshaling of resources "Desert Shield." Its goal is to protect other Arab countries such as Saudi Arabia and Egypt, as well as Israel,*

*from possible attack. Over 100,000 U.S. troops will be
flying to the region in enormous C-5 transport planes,
while aircraft carriers and other warships are stream-
ing into the Red Sea.*

One hundred thousand troops. One of them will be
Mom. I stare at the TV. The C-5 plane is huge, as big
as the football field behind the high school. They
show it loading. The front of it opens up, and big trucks
and tanks drive right inside. How can something so
big and heavy fly in the air? Why couldn't Mom fly in
a plane for people? I hate to think of her in that thing.
If they fill the plane with tanks and trucks and weapons, how can the soldiers fit? There aren't any seats inside.

"Hey!" Danielle is at the back door.

I leap up and run to open it.

"So! Tell me about Saturday. Sorry I couldn't call you.
We went to New Hampshire for the weekend. What
time did your mom leave?"

"Really early. Six o'clock in the morning. We had to
go to the bus station in Portland. It was so terrible.
Everyone was crying."

Danielle hugs me.

"My mom sent you this."

It's a free ice cream cone coupon to Golly Polly's ice
cream.

"Thanks. How was the mall?" I ask.

"Great. It was really fun. We went to the arcade and

then had pizza. And we went to a movie. It was awesome."

I nod. I can't believe I'm jealous, but I am. Besides, at some point I should go to the mall. I have to get some stuff for school.

"Hey, how's Jake?"

"He's . . . he's . . ." Now I start to cry. I'm not tough. I'm a marshmallow. I wonder if Mom cried on that big ugly C-5 airplane.

"What?" Danielle asks. "What happened?"

"He went to work, right? But he doesn't get out until six at night. He works from ten till six, and so he wants me to go get Andrew with the stroller. I'll have to leave practice by four-thirty."

"You can't do that! You're the captain. Coach will go ballistic!"

"Yeah, I know. I tried to explain, but you know Jake. I can't talk to him about anything. He just left and told me that's what I have to do."

"No, it isn't. I'll talk to my mom," Danielle says. "She'll pick up Andrew for you. I know she will. Jake doesn't understand about practice is all. Maybe she can explain to him that if you miss practice, you're in big trouble."

"No, Danielle, don't talk to your mother about this. Please?"

"Why?"

"Because. Mom only left Saturday. And if you tell, then your mom's going to think things are going badly here, and then maybe someone will call my father in Japan. I'm not kidding, Danielle. They already did that once. Jake told my mom to because he didn't want to take care of me. But I'm not going to Japan, Danielle. I'm staying here even if I have to run away."

"Wow, Jas. We *have* to tell my mom. I know she'll help you today. She loves emergencies. She's making you guys a macaroni and cheese casserole for tonight."

I heave a big sigh of relief. Danielle sits down at the table. I go to the refrigerator and pour us both Pepsis and blow my nose a couple of times. She's thinking hard now.

"Okay. You have to be our team captain. Can you imagine how bossy and show-offy Bridget would be? Oh my God, we'd kill her. It would be terrible for team morale."

"It'll be great if your mom can get Andrew today, but what about tomorrow?"

"Okay, tomorrow too. But then we'll say that Jake is getting his hours changed at work."

"You mean he'd take an earlier shift?"

"Uh, yeah. Is there one?"

"There is, but Jake doesn't like to get up early. He likes to sleep in."

"Well, too bad. You mean he'd be willing to send you to Japan so he wouldn't have to get up early?"

"I guess so," I say softly as I realize that's partly true. "But the real reason is he just wants Andrew, not me."

"That's awful, Jas. That is so unfair."

Danielle's stubborn lower jaw is set. She's frowning, and with her hands she's folding and refolding a piece of paper she found on the table.

"I'm going to have my mother give Jake a lecture. He better learn to be a parent and quick. Now come on, let's go practice. Know where your ball is?"

I run to my bedroom closet and unearth my ball and the pump, in case it needs air. In June, Mom dug a hole, and we mixed our own cement. We have our own hoop at the end of the driveway. Basically we have to play in the street, but there are almost never cars, except for slow-moving tourists looking for unmarked beaches.

The hoop is one reason the Parnells yell at us. Sometimes when the ball rolls out of bounds, it heads near their asparagus and marigolds. Then Muffy goes crazy, yipping her little brains out.

"Want to play Horse to warm up?" I ask.

"Sure. But we have to practice layups, too. I missed almost every single one the other night."

"Yeah, but you were great on defense." Danielle is so quick.

First we try a little defense. As soon as I crouch down, my knees let me know it.

"Ooof. Do your knees ache, Danielle?"

"No. You know what I have? Blisters. One on my heel and a long skinny one on the outside of my foot where my socks were bunched up."

I reach out and snag the ball from Danielle. It flips

into the air and bounces one high bounce, then starts rolling down the hill toward the Parnells'.

Muffy sees it at once. "Yap! Yap, yap, yap!"

Mr. Parnell straightens up from weeding his asparagus. Mrs. Parnell is picking flowers. I see her straw hat tilt up as she glances at us.

"Uh-oh," I mutter, remembering the famous Muffy vs. owl incident Danielle and I witnessed last winter.

Muffy is a really small dog. And one day a huge white snowy owl staked her out. The owl sat up in the big maple tree. Day after day the owl sat without moving. The Audubon Society came. The newspapers came. TV-3 came. Nobody could figure out what it was doing up there. Pretty soon everybody forgot about it, except me. But the owl was up there for two whole weeks.

Then, late one afternoon, after school, Mrs. Parnell was bringing some grocery bags from her car into the house, when suddenly the owl swooped down and grabbed Muffy in its claws.

The owl picked up Muffy and started to fly off with her. Mrs. Parnell ran out shrieking, running around the yard, flapping a dishtowel at the owl. The owl held on for a little while, but it was having trouble gaining altitude. Finally, it dropped Muffy. Muffy fell about fifteen feet, but she landed in a snowbank the Parnells' plow had pushed up, and didn't get hurt.

For days afterward, we played at being Mrs. Parnell with the dishtowel.

Together Danielle and I pound down the hill just as

the ball is rolling onto the grass, heading for the jumbo-sized Golden Queen marigolds alongside the asparagus bed. The Parnells use the marigolds to ward off slugs and cutworms.

Gasping for air, Danielle says, "Hi, Mr. Parnell. Hi, Mrs. Parnell. Hi, Muffy. Sorry about the ball. Is it okay if I get it?"

"I'll get it," says Mr. Parnell, ambling after it.

"How has Muffy been since her adventure with the owl, Mrs. Parnell?" Danielle says.

Oh my God, is she laying it on. I could never do this.

"You mean last winter?"

"Yes."

"She's fine, but I'm not sure Mr. Parnell ever quite believed I was telling the truth."

"But we saw it happen. We saw the owl grab her and everything!"

"Well, there you are, Clarence. Two eyewitnesses. Would you girls like a cookie?" Mrs. Parnell is smiling, pleased as Punch.

"We don't want to bother you," Danielle says, "but we'd love a cookie. Your zinnias are beautiful."

"Aren't they? It's been a good year for zinnias, no doubt about that. I'm making an arrangement for the library. Hold on while I go get some cookies."

I look at Danielle and roll my eyes. She grins and kneels down by the basket of zinnias. Red, hot pink, golden yellow—all double-blossomed and full.

Mrs. Parnell comes out with four cookies.

"Saw your mother leaving for the bus the other day," Mr. Parnell says. "Real early. Six o'clock."

"We said goodbye to her the night before," Mrs. Parnell says. "She came to tell us she was leaving."

I nod and bite off half my cookie. It's a hermit spice cookie with fat raisins.

"Were you a soldier? Were you in a war?" Danielle asks Mr. Parnell suddenly, making her eyes widen.

"I was in World War II. Couldn't let Hitler conquer the world, could you? Everybody went. Not like now. No one wants to defend their country. Everybody pitched in during World War II. They didn't send women, though."

"What are you talking about, Clarence, you old fool? I went. Not as a soldier, but I was closer to the front than you ever were. I was a nurse with the Red Cross. In France for two years. All the work and none of the glory."

Glory? I don't understand what she means.

"Well, thanks for the cookies," Danielle says.

I take the ball from Mr. Parnell. "Yeah, thanks."

"Say," says Mrs. Parnell, "why don't you girls come use our pool next summer? Nobody's swimming in it these days except frogs."

"Sure! Thanks," I say, and Danielle grins at me in triumph.

Back in my driveway, I ask, "So what was that all about?"

"I'm planning ahead. You should be friendlier with people, Jas. You might need their help someday."

"Help with what?"

"I don't know. What if you get locked out of the house or something? The O'Neills are never home. They're useless as neighbors."

I wish I had Danielle's confidence, but I don't. We play for over an hour, but then Danielle gets her bike and heads home so she can talk to her mother before practice. She tells me to bring the stroller when I walk over to meet her. That way her mother can have it if she needs it.

After Danielle leaves, I feel completely alone. I lie on the prickly grass in the backyard and stare at the sky. Don't fall. Please, gigantic airplane, stay in the sky. Keep my mom safe.

# 11

At last I'm at practice, and I can't wait to get started. I grab a ball and go out on the court by myself. Make a basket, leap for the rebound. Then shoot from the new spot. Make it. Leap for the rebound. I don't even know anyone else is in the gym.

Just as I go for a rebound, someone cuts in from my

right and snatches the ball from under my nose. Bridget.

"Ball hog," she says.

"Go get your own ball," I tell her. "Give that back."

"There aren't any more good ones, for your information."

She shoots, misses. We both run for the rebound. I get it. She snatches it away.

"What's your problem?" I ask. "Just take the stupid ball. I don't care."

"You were supposed to bring music for warm-ups. Remember? We asked if we could warm up with music?"

"Oh yeah." I dimly remember that. "I guess I assumed Danielle would take care of it for me."

"Well, team captains don't 'assume' stuff like that. We always had music at Red Star. It was awesome. I play so much better that way. You are so out of it, Jas. I deserve to be captain, and you know it. Everybody knows it. Coach just let you be captain because he feels sorry for you."

Bridget's crazy. When Coach picked me, he didn't know anything about Iraq. Neither did I.

I want to punch her. Kick her. Pound her little spoiled brat pea brain into the ground. But I hear Mom's voice. "Cool it, Jas. Count to ten or even one hundred if you have to. Don't let her get to you."

Coach Campbell blows his whistle. All balls have to be held immediately so he can have quiet. Or else you have to run suicides, which means sprinting the length of the court so many times in a row.

Bridget stands near me. Then she drops the ball so that it bounces off my foot and rolls away.

"Williams," Coach says without looking up, "ten suicides."

Bridget laughs silently. I glare at her. She is such a pain. I trot over to a corner of the gym and get started. I run until my lungs burn, which I think is around eight laps. I bend over, hands on my knees, to take a break.

Coach sees me. "Okay. Come on back. That's enough," he says.

We practice layups for nearly an hour. Now Danielle is practically in tears. She keeps missing. Then we do dribbling skills. Most of the girls hate it.

Coach Campbell's barking out the orders today, that's for sure. "Drive the ball forward when you run. The ball is pulling you down the court, you're not following after it. Drive it! Be aggressive. Your offense has to be aggressive."

I'm aggressive. Look at me, Coach. You want to see aggressive? I'm running circles around most of the other kids, even Bridget with her $1,000 sports camp training. I'm flying right over the tops of her fingers when I shoot.

Around four-thirty, from the corner of my eye, I catch sight of Danielle's mother. She comes in with Andrew and Stevie. She carries Andrew up the bleachers, sits down with him in her lap, and tries to pull Stevie down next to her.

"Hey! What's up, Jas? Line up on the paint for foul shots. Let's go!" Coach yells.

I guess I didn't hear him the first time. Stevie is running up and down the bleachers, which rattle noisily under his weight. Danielle's mother lifts Andrew and tries to intercept Stevie with one hand to calm him down.

"Hey! You ever hear of a rebound, Jasmyn Williams?" Coach yells at me.

"Yeah."

"Come on, Bigfoot," Bridget yells.

"Shut up, Bridget."

My eyes fill with tears. Bigfoot's a silly nickname; I've been called it so many times that it doesn't really hurt anymore. It's just that since Mom left, I don't seem to have any control over my tears. They come whenever they want. I look down at the floor, trying to blink them away, trying to ignore everyone, especially Andrew and Stevie.

I think the other girls are mad at Coach for picking on me. They know Mom is gone, and that Stevie and Andrew are here, and that I'm afraid I won't be able to make practice for the rest of the summer because it sure is clear to all us girls that Mrs. Roberge has her hands full. Maybe Bridget's right, Jake too, that I shouldn't take on the responsibility of being captain right now. She was right about my bringing the music for warm-ups. With so much going on the past few days, I just forgot.

"Where's your concentration? What's wrong with you, anyway?" Coach says.

"Nothing." Without Mom, I don't know anything. I don't even know why I'm here.

"All right. Now focus, Williams, focus. Get your head up. You have teammates, you know. So be aware of them. Play as a team member, not a soloist. Bridget, you're up next. Be ready. Bend your knees, Jas, flex 'em. Loosen up. Eye on the backboard. Loose wrist."

Six out of ten. Not bad. Not good. Now Bridget steps to the line. No doubt about it. Hoop camp did wonders for her foul shooting. It shows in how smoothly she bounces the ball as she sets up for her foul shot.

"Keep shooting, Bridget. Keep shooting till you miss. The rest of you, count 'em out loud. Six. Seven . . ."

Concentration. I'm not that good at foul shots. I'm not even as good as Danielle at getting my ball out of the Parnells' asparagus.

Suddenly there's a loud scream from the bleachers. Loud crying. My heart thuds in panic, and I look over. Andrew has fallen. Mrs. Roberge is trying to grab hold of Stevie.

"Oh, Jesus!" I yell, full of guilt and fear, and take off running. "Andrew!"

Why wasn't I watching him? I knew Mrs. Roberge had to watch Stevie, but I didn't care. I wanted to go to basketball, no matter what. Andrew is flat on his face, lying forward over the bleacher seat. Mrs. Roberge scoops him up and tries to scramble after Stevie, who is heading across the gym at top speed for the lobby door. I leap up the steps, take Andrew, and hug him close. He's howling.

"It's okay, Andrew. It's okay, little pumpkin guy."

He's such a good baby, I can't bear for him to be hurt. I bury my face in his soft neck.

"Mama?" he says.

"No, Andrew. It's me. Jas."

"Oh, Jas. I'm sorry," Mrs. Roberge is saying. "Stevie wanted to play with Andrew. He tried to pull Andrew out of my arms. I've got to go get him."

"All set?" a voice calls out.

I look down at the gym floor. Coach is standing there in his gray sweatshirt and nylon pants, whistle around his neck. The gym lights gleam on his bald head. He's waiting for me. He's actually waiting for me. He thinks I can go on with practice. Is he crazy?

Carefully I carry Andrew down from the bleachers. "I have to go home, Coach. I'm sorry."

Andrew's stroller is in the corner of the gym by the water fountain. The walk across the shiny yellow floor takes forever. I can hear the loud hum of the ventilator, the whirr of the big ceiling fans. Behind me it's dead quiet. I know Coach is furious. I carry Andrew over and strap him in. He grabs his Binky to his face and settles quickly into the curve of the canvas seat.

I kneel in front of him. "We're going home, Andrew. You won't have to go play at Stevie's house anymore. I promise."

I can see a red mark above his eyebrow that will probably turn into a bruise. I wish I had ice to put on it. Ice keeps the swelling down, and that makes bruises smaller.

Out in the corridor, Mrs. Roberge drags Stevie over to me and makes him apologize for pulling at Andrew. I nod. She hands me a canvas tote bag with a small casserole dish in the bottom, covered with plastic wrap. "This is for supper. But you need to reheat it. Do you know how to use the microwave?"

I nod.

"Are you sure? Because if you don't, I'll come right over. You leave the plastic wrap on, and reheat it for three or four minutes. But no tinfoil, right?"

"Yes, I know. Thank you."

"Okay. Danielle told me she was hoping I would talk with Jake," Mrs. Roberge says, still holding Stevie's hand as he yanks and twists to get away.

"She thought that would be a good idea. Because, I mean, Jake has never been in charge before. So we were hoping you could give him some pointers."

"I'll be happy to talk to him. Have him call me. I'm sorry, Jas, but I really can't take Andrew in the late afternoons. Maybe one of the day-care teachers could take him home with her."

"Until six?" I gasp. "Oh, no. That wouldn't be good."

"Well, I'll call and see if we can't think of something, so don't worry anymore."

"Mrs. Roberge, do you think I should quit being team captain?"

"Of course not. Now, don't worry quite so much. I'll call around eight or so."

Feeling a little better, I push the stroller up Main Street. I would like it if I didn't have to worry so much. But I don't think that's going to be the case anytime soon.

I pass the Mosswood Cemetery, our tiny excuse of a library, the gas station, the ice cream shop, the post office, Ken's Hardware.

I want to beat Stevie up for hurting Andrew. At school, he takes medicine to keep him calm, but he's not allowed to take the medicine at home, and after being calm all day, he goes nuts and has tantrums. Summers he's mostly off medication and even harder to control. But I don't care. He should know that you don't hurt babies.

Then I wonder how many babies were hurt in Kuwait. I think of that little British boy, Stuart. And how scared he is. There must be babies in Kuwait and other little kids. The Iraqi army hurt and killed so many people. And my mom has gone to help them. For a second, I understand why she went. That's what I have to remember. When she's done helping them, she'll come back.

# 12

I reheat the macaroni for dinner, and Andrew eats like a hungry little piglet, shoveling it in with his fists. Soon there is hardly any more. After eating what's left, I'm still hungry, so I stand in the middle of the kitchen for about ten minutes, feeling sorry for myself. But you can't put sorry on a plate.

I solve my problem by eating instant oatmeal. I open a pack and mix it with hot water. It seems a little gross at first—I know there aren't any vegetables in it—but it fills my stomach quickly. Then we have chocolate ice cream. Andrew ducks away from the little spoon I try to feed him with and eats the ice cream with his fists.

The chocolatey mess is unbelievable! I run to turn on the bathwater. Then I lift him out of his high chair and carry him nonstop into the bathroom. I have to get him into the tub before he goops up anything else. But as I take off his clothes, he keeps trying to scoot out the door behind me, laughing his great big laugh. I realize at that moment that I have chocolate ice cream in my hair.

"Andrew!" I yell. "Stop it! Hold still, will ya?"

Andrew plunks down on his bottom and looks up at me. He didn't like me yelling at him. I guess he thought we were playing. His face wrinkles up, and his lower lip starts to quiver. "Mama?" he says. "Mama?" He tries to crawl to the door.

"No. No Mama. Andrew, let's throw things in the tub, okay? Come on."

He crawls to the tub and stands up, tossing in a cup. I leap up and try to stow his messy clothes in the clothes hamper. When I turn around, before I can stop him, he tosses a big bath towel in the tub, and now he's got an extra roll of toilet paper that he heaves in. I lunge forward, but in it goes. I pull out a huge pulpy pink mess of dripping paper. I have no idea what to do with it. Finally I toss it and the towel in the sink and lift Andrew into the bath, where he splashes happily, slapping the water over and over again until I am thoroughly soaked. So are the walls.

How on earth did Mom do this every day? How about Mrs. Roberge with Stevie? He's been splashing around like this for ten years! I'm ready to scream. It is kind of funny, especially the soggy toilet paper, but I'm too tired and worn out to laugh.

When Jake gets home at six-thirty, Andrew and I are lying on the living-room floor watching the sports channel.

"How's everything?" he asks.

"Terrible."

Unfortunately, Jake heads first for the bathroom, and

I remember that I forgot to clean up after Andrew's bath.

"Whoa!" Jake hollers. "What happened in here? Did a tornado touch down or what?"

"I gave Andrew a bath," I mutter. Then I add, "I'd like to see you do better."

Jake comes back into the living room. "What was that?"

"I said, I'd like to see you do better."

"You think I can't take care of Andrew?"

"That's right. That's what I think."

Jake crouches down. "Hey. What's that bruise on Andrew's head all about?"

I give a huge sigh, trying to tell him by sighing not to bother me, because I did my best. "Stevie Roberge knocked him down in the bleachers at basketball practice."

"You mean you took Andrew to basketball practice? What are you, crazy? Now, you listen to me . . ." Jake bends over Andrew and pushes back his soft carroty hair to look at the bump. "Didn't anybody put ice on this, for Christ's sake?"

"I'm sorry, okay? I was trying, and don't tell me what to do, Jake. You're not my dad. You're only Andrew's dad."

Why can't he say I'm sorry your mom's not here? Or I know how hard you tried to help out today. Or even just plain thanks.

"That 'dad' stuff is garbage, Jas, and you know it. I'm

here for both of you. And while I am, you'll have to listen to me."

"Oh yeah? If you were my dad, you would make sure I got to practice. I'm captain. Don't you understand that? You'd change your work hours so I could go. That's what Mom would do. And I wouldn't have to beg her."

"Well, I told you this morning, you're not in a position to be captain." Jake heads for the refrigerator. "What's for dinner?"

Me? He's asking me that?

"I don't know."

"Well, let me ask this, then. What did you have?"

"Oatmeal. Chocolate ice cream."

"Come on, Jas, couldn't you do better than that?"

"Mrs. Roberge sent a macaroni and cheese casserole, but Andrew ate a ton of it. Hey, did you pack him a lunch for day care?"

Jake looks puzzled. "Lunch?"

"Yeah, you have to put his lunch in his diaper bag."

"Uh-oh."

Oh God. Jake is clueless. No wonder Andrew ate so much for dinner.

Speaking of clueless, before I get kicked out as captain, I want to try to remember the music for practice tomorrow. I crawl across the floor to our tapes and paw through them, looking for break-dancing stuff. Maybe Coach will keep me on. Maybe he'll feel sorry for me and let me be captain even if I miss some games. I know he didn't pick me out of pity (we didn't realize Mom was leaving then), but I wouldn't mind if he kept me for that reason.

"Mrs. Roberge is going to call around eight tonight."

"Really? And what's she going to say?" Jake asks sarcastically. He comes in eating a peanut butter and jelly sandwich, his second of the day.

Walking to the front window, I look out. The O'Neills are walking up from the cove with Alfonse on a long leash. He sniffs happily at the weeds along the street. From her back porch, Muffy yips and yaps.

"Come here, big guy." Jake gathers Andrew up and sits him in the high chair with a Popsicle, then hunches down, looking in the refrigerator for something else to eat. He pulls out a floppy slice of leftover pizza and puts it in the microwave. I go back to the sofa, rest my head on my drawn-up knees.

Jake comes over to the sofa and sits by me for a minute. I don't look at him.

"I'm sorry, Jas. Of course I'll talk to Mrs. Roberge."

"I can't give up being captain," I whisper.

He frowns a little. "Do you really think it's a good idea for your coach and your team to have a captain that can't give one hundred percent? How does that help your team?"

I shrug. I don't want to answer that.

Suddenly there's banging at the back door. "Hello?" Then I hear, "Hey, Williams, open up!" It's Shawn and his mother.

"Come on in!" I push the screen door open wide.

"Homemade baked beans," Mrs. Doucette announces.

"Praise the Lord. You could not have come at a better time," Jake says, taking the casserole, and it's obvious that he means it. "Hope you don't mind if I help myself."

I step out on the back deck with Shawn while the adults talk.

"I went down to your practice to look for you," he says, "but you weren't there."

I make a face. "I had to leave early. Andrew fell down and bumped his head. Listen, things here aren't going that great . . ."

"Sure. That's what my mother guessed. That's why she made you guys some food. Hey, I've been watching the news a little. Did your mom fly over there on one of those C-5 transport planes?"

I nod. "I think so."

"Wow. Those planes are unbelievably huge. The size of a football field. I saw one on TV. You can park six buses inside there."

I smile at him. "I was really scared to have my mom fly in one of those things."

"No wonder."

"Thanks for bringing the beans. Andrew ate all of Mrs. Roberge's casserole, and Jake couldn't find anything else to eat."

"It's okay."

"You know what happened?" I tell him then. I guess because he's really and truly been thinking about my mom, I feel I can trust him. "Bridget went into my room without asking me and took your card and went around showing it to Amy and Danielle and making fun of it. I wanted to tell you first, you know, in case you hear anything. I told her the card was one of your jokes . . ."

"You told her that?"

"Yeah."

"But it wasn't. It wasn't a joke."

"Yeah, I know." For one second, we look at each other, and my stomach lurches.

Then it's over. In the next flash, Shawn says, "So anyway, there was this panda who liked to eat out at restaurants a lot, but only Chinese restaurants, of course, and . . ."

I start to laugh. He's told me this joke before. This time I laugh because I'm happy.

The three-way phone call from Mrs. Roberge with me and Jake on different extensions doesn't actually solve anything, but at least Jake and I get to talk about a schedule without screaming at each other.

Mrs. Roberge's idea of how to solve the day-care problem is to ask the Parnells for help. If they could go pick up Andrew at four forty-five, then I could get him from their house right after practice. But I'd still be alone with him until seven, and I still couldn't go to away games. Besides, I don't think the Parnells could

99

keep up with Andrew. I think Jake should change his hours. And Jake thinks I should quit being captain. No one will compromise.

After ten minutes of this, I suggest we all hang up because Mom might be trying to call us.

"Oh, Jasmyn, honey, I don't think so," Mrs. Roberge says. "Not yet, anyway. Maybe she'll have more of a chance tomorrow."

After he hangs up, Jake sits down at the kitchen table and starts a list of people who could help with Andrew. So far he has me, himself, and Mrs. Roberge on it. Then he gets stuck. "Do you know the Parnells pretty well?"

"Kind of, yeah, but there's no way they could— I mean, they don't have kids."

"Honest to God, how does your mom do this, Jas?" he mutters. "How on earth does she manage to go to work? You must know. Come on, Jas. You see her; she just zooms around here like it's nothing."

"You think I know? Go look in the bathroom."

"Yeah. You did pretty bad in there. You better get that picked up."

"Are you going to help me?"

"Yeah. I will. In a minute."

But with Jake, minutes are very, very long, and I am just finishing as he comes in to help.

# 13

The next morning is no easier. Andrew won't stop crying on and off, about every fifteen minutes. I think he's looking for Mom. He stops what he's doing and looks around, then starts to fuss and sometimes howl. His face is red as a beet, he's been crying so long. I try to hug him, but he pushes me away and cries harder.

One thing that doesn't help is having Jake dress him. Mom makes it a big game, playing with his toes and stuff, but Jake is all business, shoving his arms and legs around into the little arm- and legholes.

"What's wrong with him, Jas? Do you think he's sick? His tooth has popped through. Should I call the doctor?"

"I don't think so. Maybe you should wait a while and see if he gets worse. Anyway, it's after nine-thirty. You still have to pack his lunch, remember?"

"Oh, Jesus. That's right."

"He likes hard-boiled eggs. And apple slices he can chew on."

"Oh yeah. Do we have any apples?"

"No." I'm glad Andrew had a good breakfast.

"I need a plastic container." Jake hunts for one.

Andrew lets out a squawk.

"Here, Andrew. A Popsicle. Don't drip, all right? Where's that stupid diaper bag? Come on, Jas! Help me look, dammit!"

"Don't swear. Nobody's allowed to in this house."

"Okay, okay. Sorry. Get me some clean overalls and a T-shirt, then. Here. Here's the bag. Andrew, buddy, eat that Popsicle a little faster. It's dripping all over the place."

"He's supposed to have his own supply of baby wipes, too."

"What? Oh. Where are they?"

"Bathroom."

"Come on, Jas. Can you get them?"

"Yeah. Maybe." I like having a little power.

I trot down the hall to Andrew's room, but he's out of T-shirts. They must all be down in the dryer. I've lost track of the laundry situation. Oh well. I grab the wipes and run back to the kitchen.

"All his clean shirts are still in the dryer. Hey, do you think Mom will call today?"

"Today? I doubt it." With one hand, Jake is trying to throw some baked beans into a plastic dish to take to work. In the other hand, he's got the diaper bag.

"Okay. Diapers, wipes, bottle. What else? Lunch. Oh, the kid."

He reaches for Andrew. "I really hate this."

"Wait!" I yelp. "Who's picking him up?"

"You are. Now, come on, Jas, deal with it. I have to go." He steps out onto the back deck. "Quit overreacting."

Then I snap. "You know what? You know how stressed out you feel right now? That's exactly how I feel about basketball. That's exactly one hundred percent how I feel!"

I'm going to miss part of practice again! It's over. Completely over. My sports career, my college scholarship, everything is ruined. I slam the door shut after him as hard as I can.

The door opens again instantly. Jake has his finger in my face. "You listen to me, young lady. Don't you ever, ever slam a door on me again. You got that?"

I nod.

"Good." He stomps down the stairs with Andrew.

At that same moment, I see Bridget and Amy riding their bikes down my street at full speed, and right behind them is my best friend.

"Get your ball, Jas, so we can practice," Bridget calls. "Oh, hi." She waves to Jake as he backs out. "Andrew! Hi, Andrew. Look at him. He's so cute."

I toss them the ball and then sit on the back steps while they warm up a little.

Danielle hunches down next to me. "What's wrong?"

"Nothing. I have a headache."

"Hey, did your mom call yet?" Danielle asks.

"No. She will, though."

"Come on." Danielle yanks me to my feet. I go out on the street, and it's one of those days when anger makes you perfect, and everything I touch turns to steel.

I remember to bring to practice the tapes and my little tape deck, which I carry in my gym bag. I also have to lug the stroller. So I get there about two minutes late, and then I leave at four forty-five to go get Andrew. As I'm heading across the court, Coach jogs over to me.

"You're getting your baby brother, right? After you pick him up, can you stop in on your way home for a minute? I want to talk to you alone."

I freeze and glance at his face. His voice is completely neutral and already he's running back to practice. Coach lives and dies for basketball. What can he want to say to me—except that I should quit being team captain?

At day care, I shove Andrew into the stroller, grab his diaper bag, and hurry back up Main Street.

"Hey! Williams! Wait up!" Shawn is pedaling wildly across the school parking lot. He pulls up next to me and gets off his bike. "Sorry I missed your practice. Aren't you going home now?"

"Coach wants to talk to me about something."

"Uh-oh."

"Yeah. Can't be good."

The other girls are just coming out. Danielle is busy talking and barely waves to me. My heart sinks. I was counting on her to come with me.

"I'll wait in the hall for you," Shawn offers. "I'll watch Andrew." He takes the stroller and starts racing down the hall with it. Andrew shrieks with delight. "Vrrooom. Vrooom. Hang on, Andrew, you dude. Ready, set, go!"

Inside the gym, Coach is locking up the equipment closet and shutting off the lights with a special key.

"Oh, hi, Jas. Glad you stopped by. Listen, I know there's a lot going on at home right now. But, to tell you the truth, I didn't know that when I appointed you captain. Here. Sit down here on the bleachers for a second."

I sit on the bleachers. I guess people ask you to sit down when they're going to give you bad news, as if they're worried that you might pass out or something.

"You know how I make it a rule that everyone on the team gets the same treatment. For example, if you miss a practice, you don't start the next game, even if you're a superstar, right?" he asks.

I nod. This is it. The big chop. The ax is about to fall. I feel two hot bright spots burn on my cheeks. I'm sitting in a hunched-up little knot.

"One of the families complained last night . . ."

"Bridget's," I say bitterly.

"They said you'll have to modify your schedule, with your mother away and all, and you have a lot of extra responsibilities now that the other kids don't have . . ."

Exactly! I yell inside my head. So don't take this one good thing away from me!

"But a captain needs to be able to give more than a hundred percent to her team, to set an example at all times, to motivate, and so on. Right?"

I nod.

"Well, I didn't think it was fair to take away your position since I just gave it to you."

I look up at him.

"Also because of your talent and because you do set a great example for the kids. So what I thought I'd do, in an effort to be fair to everybody, is make two co-captains. You and Bridget. Sound good?"

Share with Bridget? He's got to be kidding. Co-captains? I try to smile. He means well. I guess.

"So you and Bridget are co-captains for the Pre-season League. And then, well, we'll take it from there."

I still sit like a lump of wet towel. It isn't until Coach claps me on the shoulder that I realize he's finished talking with me. "You get on home now. Sorry I had to keep you."

"Okay, Coach. No problem."

Out in the cool, shadowy hallway, I take Andrew and his stroller from Shawn.

"What'd he want?" Shawn asks. I don't feel much like talking about it. My thoughts are pretty jumbled up.

"Oh, nothing. I'll see you tomorrow maybe. Or the next day. Thanks for watching Andrew."

All the way home, I think over the conversation with Coach. Come to think of it, he sounded like Jake, about a team captain giving more than a hundred percent. But I *do* give it all I have. As soon as practice starts, I put every ounce of effort and ability I have into it. Isn't that the point? Besides, didn't Coach warn us not to go running home to our parents to complain? Now that Bridget has done that and gotten her way, maybe she'll be even more spoiled and obnoxious. It's like giving her permission to treat me like dirt, while she gets to flash her little MVP T-shirt around.

MVP. I have to smile a little. I know what Shawn would say about those initials. Most Valuable Pain. Well, there's nothing I can do about that. If she wants to be a show-off and a dweeb, that's her choice.

On the other hand, maybe Jake and Coach are right. Maybe it isn't fair to the other kids that I can't be around all the time but still get to be captain. What's so fair about that?

Andrew and I pass the cemetery and the ice cream shop. As usual, Andrew twists around in his stroller and begs for ice cream. The light breeze cools my face. Walking is relaxing. It gets you thinking in a way that doesn't happen when you're sitting in cars. The Parnells drive by and honk. I wave back.

I sigh. Actually, to my surprise, I feel a little relieved to have the pressure of being captain lifted off me. I'd always be worrying about making a game, especially now that I know how much Andrew needs me. I'm pretty sure Bridget will be at basketball every single minute. So if I do have to help out at home, the team will still have a captain.

By the time Andrew and I get home, I'm feeling pretty cool. Except for the Bridget part. She still drives me nuts.

That night, after Andrew's bath, we're all three of us sitting around on the floor of the living room. Jake is letting Andrew climb on his stomach and then bounce up and down on him until he falls over laughing. Then he gets up and does it again. Andrew's such a clown.

Jake missed the news, so he reaches over Andrew and clicks on the TV. I groan.

"What?" Jake asks.

"Can you turn that off? I saw it earlier."

He shrugs. "Okay."

We sit there, watching Andrew flop around. I'm arguing with myself about whether to bring up that Coach has changed me to co-captain. It's like losing a great big argument, which Jake will think he won. And if Jake starts saying "I told you so," I'll have a fit.

"Gotta give my ribs a little rest, buddy." Still lying on his back, Jake lifts Andrew in the air and waves him around like an airplane. Looks like fun.

In the end, I can't help myself. Out it comes.

"So, Jake, guess what happened at practice today. Coach made me and Bridget co-captains. We're going to share the job in case I have to leave early once in a while, or something."

"Oh yeah? Hey, that sounds pretty good, sharing it, don't you think?"

"Yeah. I guess it's okay." I smile at him and shrug.

"Well, cool."

"Sometime you gotta meet Bridget. She complained about me. Just meet her once. Then you'll get the full picture."

I guess he's not going to say "I told you so." Good.

"Oooof. Hey, Andrew! Take it easy, buddy. You're breaking my ribs again. Here. Go push this truck around. Well, I'm glad your coach thought of that. To compromise."

"Yeah, I guess, but it doesn't make anybody really happy."

"Nope. But you know what? I bet that other girl, Bridget, I'll bet she's far less happy than you about sharing it."

"Yeah, you're right." I have to smile. She probably thought that if she complained, Coach would throw me out altogether. "So . . . I mean . . . did you think about changing your hours at all?" I ask, hoping he won't get mad.

He doesn't answer right away. Uh-oh, I'm thinking. Maybe he's going to blow up at me again. But he's the one who mentioned compromise. I hold my breath.

"Yeah, of course I did. I thought about it," he says.

I start to feel half miserable again. I'm not asking him any more questions, that's for sure. Maybe I've learned you can push Jake only so far.

"All right, Jas. You know what? This co-captain thing makes it a little easier for me. At least I know if I need you to get Andrew, it won't be such a big deal. I'll call the night shift supervisor at the factory and tell him I want to switch my hours. I'll see what he says. Deal?" He sticks out his hand.

"Yeah. Deal." We shake. Then he smiles.

"But, Jas, do you have any idea how absolutely much I hate to get up early? I mean, we're talking six o'clock here. Nobody's up then but roosters."

# 14

The phone rings around 6 a.m. on Wednesday. I leap out of bed, hoping it's Mom. But it's Jake's supervisor from the factory.

"Can you get Jake for me?" he asks.

"Sure. In a minute."

Waking Jake up isn't easy. He sleeps dead to the world. I bang on Mom's bedroom door. "Phone! Jake, wake up!"

"All right, all right. Got it." He groans. "Hello?"

Two minutes later, he comes staggering out of the

bedroom, with his reddish hair sticking straight up like Andrew's.

"Hi, Spike," I say.

"Guess what? I got changed to the early shift. Eight to four. You happy now?"

"Oh, wow! That is so awesome, Jake. That's great!"

"Yeah. Now if you'll excuse me, you're blocking the route to the bathroom."

I'm so excited I want to call Danielle, but she doesn't get up early. I run outside in my bare feet and pj's. I prance around the yard in the cold, dewy grass and let the newly risen sun run up my arms. Two fishing boats are heading out to sea together. Today could be a great day.

But by that night, Mom still hasn't called. I sit huddled on the sofa, waiting. For nothing. Running down to do the laundry every so often. We never had so many clean socks in this house. Watching the TV news. More weapons. Troops. Charts. Fat pink generals. Saddam and his hostages. Each day looks the same.

Five days have gone by. Mom must have reached Saudi Arabia by now. She *must* have. She never did call from Spain, the way she said she would, and by now she must have been in Saudi Arabia for a day or two.

I sit there, staring out the window.

"Why doesn't she call?" I ask Jake for the millionth time.

I can't eat my supper, which is bagels on paper plates with cream cheese and tomato soup. It looks a lot like lunch did. Jake's cooking skills are at ground zero.

"Maybe the phone lines aren't set up. You have to realize, Jas, they're moving 100,000 soldiers over there as fast as they can. Your mom's in a supply battalion. She probably hasn't had a break since she got there."

"She said she'd call."

"Give her a chance, will ya? Now, come on and eat up."

Sighing, I rip off a piece of tough bagel dough and poke it in my soup. "I can't."

And then the phone does ring! I leap out of my chair, knocking it over, and dash to pick it up ahead of Jake. And it's Mom! It really is.

"Hey! Mom, why didn't you call us before? I was so worried."

"I couldn't, Jas. I honestly couldn't."

" 'Cause you're so busy?"

"Yeah. I've been working eighteen hours a day. This place is total chaos right now. Picture this. We'll be moving 330,000 gallons of jet fuel and 8,305,000 gallons of diesel fuel through here. And that's just for my unit."

"Wow."

"And the plane, the way we got here, the plane was huge, Jas. Three hundred feet long. A C-5 transport. We sat on top of all the gear on little canvas straps. Seventeen hours to Saudi."

"Yeah, they showed it on TV."

My mood shrivels like a popped balloon. It sounds as if she's having fun, as if she's off on a great adventure and doesn't need us at all.

"Did you stop in Spain?"

"Just for a few hours. For refueling. I didn't forget about calling, but there was no place to call from, Jas."

"Will you be back in time for my birthday?"

"Oh, Jas, I don't think so. But everyone says we won't be here long."

"When are they going to free Stuart?" I interrupt.

"Stuart? Who's Stuart?"

"You know, the little boy in the blue shorts. Who became a hostage. You said you'd come home after we freed Stuart. Remember?"

"Oh. Well, I bet in a month we'll know a whole lot more. The army only tells us a little bit at a time. Hey! Write me a letter. I'll give Jake the address."

"Yeah," I mumble, ashamed of how short and grumpy my letter is, how awful I was at the bus station. And now I'm jealous on top of it. Jealous of the army.

"What? I can't hear. Listen, sweetie, is Jake there? And Andrew?"

"Yeah, Jake's getting the extension. Hold on."

How can she not remember Stuart? Every time I close my eyes, I see his narrow little body in front of that row of camouflaged soldiers, Saddam pushing him forward. And he's resisting them, fighting them every step of the way.

"Hey, Paula! How are you? We miss you so much back here. We really do," Jake says.

I wish I had said that to her, that I missed her. I wanted to. But I couldn't. I can't even hear the words without feeling as if I'm going to drown in a wave of tears.

"Andrew says hi," Jake says. "He's standing here, biting the phone cord. Same as always."

"I didn't know if you'd be there at the house, Jake. It's early for you, isn't it?"

"Yeah, well, I got my hours changed right away. The boss was pretty nice about it. So we're surviving. Mostly anyway."

"Let me give you that overseas address. Got a pencil?" She reads off an APO address. "Listen, I can't talk long. I waited two and a half hours to get to the phone. The person behind me is about to strangle me."

"Paula, just one more question. So, uh, what exactly are the living arrangements out there?"

"Living arrangements? Well, we're most of us in tents. The sand is pretty hard-packed, hard enough to drive a tent peg into. We can drive five-ton trucks on it. It's awful hot. Around one hundred twenty degrees today. It's like living in an oven. Not like Maine, that's for sure."

"No, I meant are you in a women's tent, or what?"

"Oh, I'm in a five-man tent, which in my case is four men and me. I tried to transfer, but my battalion commander wouldn't let me. Kind of lacking in privacy for all of us, but the guys are being really good about it."

"But that's not good enough, Paula . . ." Jake starts to say.

"It's better than most people have, believe me. A lot of the guys have to sleep on their jeeps and tanks because there are no more cots. Nobody wants to sleep on the ground and have a scorpion or snake run up their pant leg in the dark. Listen, I have to go. Don't panic if you don't hear from me right away. We'll get this all organized soon. Write me, Jas! You have the address now. Send me pictures! Love you!"

She hangs up. The whole house goes dead silent. I let the phone dangle by its cord. The receiver twirls in circles. I'm thinking, She likes it. She left us.

I thought I would be so glad when she called that I'd be bouncing off the walls like Stevie, but I sit there not moving. Mom isn't just gone, as in gone to the grocery store. She's in a boiling-hot desert with scorpions and tanks and huge transport airplanes and fighter jets. And now she's different, too. I don't know how to write to her.

Jake comes out of Mom's bedroom carrying Andrew. He sets him down in the middle of the living room with some plastic toys, the stackable doughnut rings, giant lock blocks. Then Jake sits down on the sofa next to me. He leans forward with his arms resting on his legs, hands drooping down. "Rough, huh?" he says.

I nod, afraid I'll start crying. I don't want Jake to hug me. We haven't been real huggy before, and I don't want to start now.

"She's pretty busy, Jas. It may be a week before she calls again. Maybe two."

"That's okay. She's going to come back soon. All the generals say so. Especially Stormin' Norman. He says it's going to be over real quick."

Jake starts to answer, then says nothing. He picks up the remote from where it's wedged between a cushion and the arm of the sofa. He clicks on the TV. First they show soldiers training at Fort Bragg, North Carolina, jumping off low-flying helicopters, wriggling in the dirt with rifles.

*The defense of Saudi Arabia and its oil remains of the utmost importance. By the end of the month, the U.S. will have 100,000 troops there to support the 30,000 advance troops who have already arrived. Here we interview townspeople as loved ones leave Berea, Kentucky. This small town has turned out in force for a big goodbye from everybody. One gas station owner says, "We'll send 'em, but we want 'em home soon. We don't want none of that Vietnam thing."*

Then the TV cameraman focuses on several other gas station owners in Berea, holding signs that say, "Just get the gas and kick their ass." The men hoot when they see the cameras and raise their fingers to make a V sign. V for victory.

Jake gives a dry snort of a laugh at the slogan. "I guess that's one way to sum it up," he says.

"What's the 'Vietnam thing'?" I ask.

"That means that back then people felt the war was dragging on forever, and nobody knew what we were fighting for."

"Oh. Well, Jake, what are we fighting for this time?"

"Well, we, I guess like they just said—to get the oil

and defeat this guy Saddam, the dictator, so he doesn't keep on going and attack his other neighbors. He's got a huge army, and the guy is completely nuts. Plus he's got those poison weapons. Chemical and biological stuff. He may even have an atomic bomb."

I freeze. A huge army? Poison weapons? I put my hands over my face. I can't stand to look at the U.S. missiles.

"Uh-oh. Darn, Jas. I'm sorry. Oh, man. Hey. I didn't mean to scare you. None of that stuff is going to happen. Your mom's not a combat soldier. This whole thing is to prevent that from happening."

I nod. But it's too late. This new knowledge has burned its way into me in one single instant. Andrew crawls over and hands me a toy. I take it without even looking at it, then set it down. I get up and go outside.

Down at the cove, the water is gray and choppy. There are small whitecaps of sea foam at the top of each wave. The beach is gray, too, cold and rocky, nearly dark. The tide is up and the beach narrow, crowded with logs, boulders, an old tire. Me. Two sailboats enter the channel with their sails down and tied, using their engines. Seagulls stalk the rocks.

Across the channel, Moorhead Island looks cold and all alone. The gray rocks around the edge are barriers. No one can cross easily to go ashore. There are silent green pine trees, pointy-topped, and regular, leafy trees already tinged slightly with orange. I don't want fall to come.

Why did Jake tell me that stuff about the weapons? I did ask, but I'm a kid. I shouldn't have to know.

But what if Jake didn't tell me? Probably I'd figure it out anyway. I mean, this Gulf War, well, it's not supposed to be really a war, but it's everywhere. In every magazine and on every TV station.

I roll the tire up, away from the splashing edge of the waves, and sit in it as though it's a lounge chair. I sit there, watching the sky grow slowly darker and little stars pop out one at a time. I sit there until the small, feeble mosquitoes of late summer drive me home.

# 15

On the day of our first game, Jake makes a big announcement before going to work. "You're not playing today unless you've written to your mother. You got that?"

Jake hasn't learned that you don't use a big, heavy threat as your first resort, your starting point for negotiations. He's got a long way to go as a parent. But I let him get away with it this time.

"I wrote once."

"Well, write again. Put some effort into it."

I get a piece of stationery, a purple marker, and plop down right away on the sofa.

*Dear Mom,*

*I am glad you are having so much fun. It doesn't sound like fun to me, but if you like it, I guess that's what counts. We have our first game today. I don't know if I told you, but a few days after you left, the coach demoted me to co-captain with Bridget. But that's okay. Jake helped me out that day, thinking about what the team needs. Andrew isn't crying anymore. I guess his teeth are fine.*

*Love, Jas*

It's mid-August, and Stuart is still trapped in the embassy building with hundreds of other people. I don't really know what an embassy is, and neither does Jake. We look it up in the dictionary, and it says an embassy is a place where you send an ambassador. I hate when the dictionary tells you the meaning of the word by using the word. Jake hates this, too.

I have been dreaming about Stuart, both daydreams and night dreams. In the daydreams, I am a soldier in charge of organizing Stuart's rescue from a Baghdad hotel. At night, I am the little boy in the blue shorts, lying on the floor, with soldiers in machine guns standing in a circle around me. They never sleep. I am always watched. They won't let me go to the men's room. They tell me to pee in a bucket, but I won't. They tell me to eat stale bread with marmalade, but I won't. I am going to die. It's better that way.

· · ·

Mom's first letters reach us on Thursday, the day of my first away game. One is for me and Andrew, one for Jake. My letter is very cheery. And short.

*Dear Jas and Pumpkin Man,*

*You won't believe this, but every single soldier over here has a cold. A cold. In the desert! A fever, a croaky sore throat that just won't quit. And it's over one hundred degrees every day. Maybe we all came down with the flu. Troops are flying in by the hundreds day and night now.*

*Everybody hates the food and says it's worse than dog food. Most of the time, we move water and dig holes. For fun we've got a volleyball tournament going. Every time I play, I think of you. How's Pre-season going? Write to me. Please? Give my favorite pumpkin a great big squeeze!*

*Love, Mom*

*P.S. Calling isn't that easy because of sandstorms and equipment problems. But I'll be sure to call on your birthday no matter what. Write me!*

I watch the news station while I wait for Danielle's mom to pick me up. Stuart is still trapped in the embassy with a bunch of other people, and Saddam, who tried to pretend he was so nice to them at first, now hardly gives them any food or water. The newsman says they're nearly starving.

Mrs. Roberge is honking in the driveway. She is driving most of the team to Scarborough for our second game. I grab my gym bag and run for the door.

The girls chatter in the car. Danielle turns on her tape deck, and they sing loudly. But I watch out the window as the fields that used to be meadows for cow farms slide by. How udderly sad.

The moment I step onto the glossy gym floors, I am changed. I feel washed clean. I am a windshield after a car wash. Invisible, but in a good and powerful way.

I bounce the ball a few times, my eyes on the rim with its soft trailing net beneath. My feet are where they need to be. Bounce, a small jump. A lift, really. The arc is like a rainbow falling through bruised clouds onto the sea islands after a storm passes by.

A three-pointer. People are clapping. Danielle tosses me the rebound.

Check my feet. A few bounces and lift. Height, an arc. A hose watering sunflowers. A scatter of clapping.

Coach comes up behind me, tugs my braid. "What's this, Williams? You got a secret weapon now?"

"Yeah." I smile. "I guess so."

"Well, don't give it away. We're in enemy territory here, don't forget."

He blasts his whistle, and we crowd around for his little pre-game pep talk. His sermon, Bridget calls it.

"This is our toughest competitor. So how are we going to win? Psychology. Attitude."

Oh my God. He's been in basic training!

"This is not a game for show-offs. It's about one thing. What's that one thing, Danielle?"

"Teamwork."

"Right."

"What's teamwork mean, Bridget?"

"Passing," she mumbles.

"Wrong. What comes before passing, Jas?"

"Looking for the open girl."

"Right. Know where your teammates are all the time. You ready?"

We put our hands into the circle and squeeze them together like spokes on a wheel. We squeeze harder and harder and then we yell, "Fight!"

And then I yell, "Free Stuart!"

Everyone stares at me as if I'm nuts.

When the score gets close at the end of the third quarter, Coach calls us all over. While we're toweling off, he says, "Danielle, we need a ten-point lead now, right? So I want everyone to feed Danielle the ball. Then, Jas, go ahead and take a three-pointer whenever you feel comfortable."

"What?" shrieks Bridget. "Only Jas gets to take three-pointers? That's not fair."

It's not fair that I'm so hot this afternoon, either. I can't miss.

We win by a lot.

We have four more games, through the week before school starts. And every time at the end of the third quarter, even though we're usually already ahead, Coach tells me to start going for the three-pointers. He loves to hear the crowd hoot and holler is why. At the home games, I can even hear Shawn whistling from his perch in the top row.

I want to have fun and be like the other girls. I try to smile and look happy. But the truth is, I feel hollow, divided into two parts. One part of me is in the desert, in fear, hot, lost, and always worried about my mom. The other part is standing here, smiling at the crowd.

# 16

September 4 comes. It's my birthday. Mom always has a few presents for me on the sofa when I come out in the morning. She calls them her tokens of appreciation. When I trot out to the sofa, there's nothing there. But it's still early.

I don't say anything at first, because it's barely 7 a.m., and Jake is busy getting Andrew into a fresh diaper and clothes, and that's a lot of work. Andrew seems to get squirmier every day.

From the kitchen, I hear Andrew's playful laugh and the *thud, thud, thud* of his little hands and knees as he crawls down the hall. Jake is in the bathroom, yelling,

"Hey, Andrew, get back in here." Every time Jake hollers, Andrew shrieks with laughter and crawls farther away. He's speedy.

I bring the newspaper from the front steps and put it on the table. Jake likes to read the overnight stuff from Saudi Arabia while he feeds Andrew breakfast.

Finally they come out of the bathroom. I'm kind of hanging out on the sofa, expectantly. "Well?" I ask.

Jake gets a bib, puts Andrew in his high chair. He places a bowl of Froot Loops on Andrew's tray, and a cup with milk beside it. But when he reaches for the lid, Andrew lifts the cup and leans over the side of his chair to watch as he carefully pours the milk on the floor.

"Can you get that?" Jake asks, his first words to me. Not "Hi, Jas. Happy birthday."

"Uh, no." He's the one who gave Andrew uncontained milk, not me.

He turns around. "You really talk this way to your mom?"

"No. She doesn't ask me such stupid questions."

"Wow. Which side of the bed did you get up on? What's wrong with you?"

"It's my birthday! See!" I snatch the calendar off the wall and shove it in front of his face. "See all those purple circles that are on the calendar so people like you won't forget? Well?"

"A well," Jake says, "is a hole in the ground."

"No. I mean, have you got any presents hanging around?" I ask.

"Presents? Ohhhh. Yeah."

He hurries back to the sink, getting sponges to clean up the milk. "Right. Eleven years old. Twelve, as of today. That's what a birthday is. Yes, sir. Couldn't find the wrapping paper last night, so . . ."

"That's okay. They don't have to be wrapped or anything."

I lean against the doorframe. The calendar from Ken's Hardware has only one photo, showing a typical New England fall scene with orange-leafed maple trees. September 4 has been circled about a billion times in purple marker.

"Listen," he says, "can you pick up Andrew at four-thirty? I have to be a touch late."

I don't have basketball anymore, so that won't be a problem. Jake probably has to go buy me a cake.

"Yeah, sure." I'm still waiting.

Anyway, Mom will call me. I know she will. I take my bowl of cereal to the TV and sit down. I don't think twice about turning on the news now. Jake and I watch it whenever we can. But then I get up and head back into the kitchen.

I glare at Jake. "Why don't you just admit it? You totally forgot my birthday, didn't you? Right?"

Something in Jake snaps. This time I've gone too far.

"Hey, fine." He throws his hands up, then grabs Andrew's diaper bag. "If you want somebody to blame for this whole mess, that's right. Go ahead and blame me.

I'm here, doing what I can, pitching in so you don't have to get sent away to Japan, and for you, for Miss Basketball Princess, I'm never good enough. Right? You make that pretty darn obvious."

He grabs the bag, scoops up Andrew, and heads out the door.

"See ya tonight," he mutters. "Don't forget to pick up Andrew."

Seconds later, I hear the VW start up and back out of the driveway. Did Jake really forget my birthday? How could he leave like that? And then a worse thought: Is *he* going to run away? I'd never thought of that before. If he did, and he took Andrew, there'd be no one to take care of me. I'd be sent to Japan for sure.

I try to push away this mound of worry and self-pity. I try not to let it win. I know Mom will call today around six. That's her calling time.

I blow my nose a bunch of times and lie down on the sofa. I try to meditate. We did it once in school to reduce stress. I breathe slowly for a few minutes, but meditating is boring.

I heave a big sigh and go out to check my garden. I drag the hose over to the sunflowers first. The yellow petals are wilting. Some are turning tan. I soak them down. Then I drag the hose over to the pumpkins. Some of the vine leaves are turning yellow. That's not good. Carefully I lift up each pumpkin to see if they're rotting where they touch the ground. They're sitting on paper plates, but still.

The Parnells are outside, bent over in their garden, doing their weeding early before it gets too sunny and hot. All of a sudden, I see them straighten up. Mrs. Parnell's holding a basket, and Mr. Parnell dumps something in it. They're heading over here! Uh-oh. I haven't been near their asparagus lately. Neither has Danielle. We haven't played Horse in weeks.

"Howdy," Mr. Parnell calls out in his raspy voice.

"Got some vegetables for you. For your birthday," Mrs. Parnell says. "It's today, right?"

"Yeah! It is." I reach out for the basketful of fresh corn, green beans, and tomatoes. After all the waffles, ice cream, and bagels, vegetables look great. "Thank you!"

"How old are you? Didn't your mother tell us you're eleven?"

"I'm twelve today. I'm going into seventh grade."

"Well, now," says Mr. Parnell, "that's fine."

"We watch the news every day," Mrs. Parnell says. "We're proud of your mother. It's not easy, what she's doing."

Tears fill my eyes. I look away, out across the cove at the ocean, flat and blue, stretching to the horizon's rim. If I were Danielle, I'd have something nice and cheery to say about the view. Instead, I get right to the point. "Do you think she'll be okay?" I ask.

"Oh, my Lord, yes," Mrs. Parnell says. "With all our new communications? And the size of the Allied forces? Except for the heat, I would imagine she's going to be fine."

"Well, thanks for the vegetables." I nod, feeling pretty awkward. "How did you know it was my birthday?"

"We asked your mother before she left. We're watching out for you, dear."

I bring the vegetables inside. I love fresh corn, especially the yellow-and-white-kerneled kind.

This is a really different birthday. Corn from the Parnells. A fight with Jake. I wish I hadn't snapped at him the way I did. Jake was nothing to me before. Just Mom's boyfriend. I never would have thought I'd care about anything he did.

I feel as if I'm on a roller-coaster ride of feelings, rattling up and down, spinning, careening almost out of control. I've been that way for a whole month.

I think of Andrew falling and bumping his soft little forehead on the bleachers. How terrible I felt at that moment. How selfish. The most important thing in the world was to protect him, and all I'd been worrying about was showing up snotty Bridget by outplaying her in Pre-season.

I remember that phone call when I listened in. It's as if I took a step outside of being a child to face this other part of my mom. It was a part I'd never had to think about.

Now I've seen bombs, jets, huge planes, and tanks. I can't just flick these visions away, flip to another channel the way Danielle can. Specialized helicopters. For destroying people. And people have already died. In Kuwait. Children. Mothers. Babies. Anyone can die in war, not just soldiers. Even camels are killed. And shore-birds. And my mother felt she had to go stop all that.

I guess sooner or later someone had to cross the ocean and help. But it didn't have to be her. Suddenly I know I have to tell her this. Not in a tearful way, and not on the phone. The calls are too confusing. I will have to write it in a letter.

First, though, I want to tell Shawn that I was right, after all, that my mother never should have left. No mother should leave her children unless she absolutely has to.

The phone rings. I dive for it, hoping it's him.

"Oh, hi, Danielle." I'm glad to hear her voice.

"Happy birthday! You finally made it to twelve."

"Yeah. Thanks."

"Listen. My mom made you some cupcakes."

"She did?"

"Yeah, for your birthday. I'll bring them over in about a half hour."

"Okay! And thank your mom for me."

After I hang up, I glance around. The house is a mess. It doesn't seem to bother Jake if things aren't picked up. I throw all the dishes in the sink and run water over them, then sponge off the table and counters. I pick up toys and newspapers and vacuum the living room.

When I hear Danielle hollering from the back door, I rush into the kitchen. She's already inside, and with her are Bridget and Amy. What! On my birthday, she brought them here? Without telling me?

"I met Bridget and Amy on Main Street," Danielle says. "I thought it would be fun if they came over." She hands me a shoebox with twelve cupcakes inside. Each one has pink icing and a pink candle. "Let's light the candles. You want to?"

"Sure."

We each have two cupcakes. As I'm sweeping the crumbs off the table and into the garbage, Bridget says, "So, Miss Co-captain, what are you going to do about Andrew when the real season starts? Leaving in the middle of practice isn't going to go over too well the second time around."

"Bridget!" says Danielle. "Come on. Cut it out."

"I guess you never noticed that I didn't miss a single Pre-season game—or much practice. Jake had his hours changed ages ago. There won't be a problem," I tell her, glancing at Danielle. I don't like where this is heading. Bridget's just jealous about my three-pointers.

"Oh yeah. Jake. Your mother's boyfriend. How could your mom go off and leave you with someone like that? I mean, they're not even married, right? He could take off maybe, one day decide to go to Las Vegas or California."

Now I'm furious. Jake, for all his faults, loves my mom, and he's honest, and he's always there for Andrew, and that's the most important thing.

My cheeks are burning. Bridget is such a jerk. In a faraway place behind a waterfall of anger and shame, I hear Danielle say, "Bridget, I can't believe you said that. Tell Jas you're sorry."

"Get out of here, Bridget!" I shout. I push her backward against the screen door.

"Hey! Leave me alone. Anyway, who would have a hick kid like Shawn for a boyfriend? Did you ever see how worn-out his sneakers are?"

"Get out!" I shove her out the door, still yelling. "Shawn's wonderful. He's worth a hundred of you. Now leave. Get out of my yard. You too, Amy."

Bridget and Amy grab their bikes and take off.

"I better go," Danielle says. "I have to get back home and watch Stevie for a while. I'll see you tomorrow. Sorry, Jas."

I nod, and they head off up the street. I sink down on the top step of the porch in tears, my head resting on my arms.

# 17

The long and terrible birthday passes. At lunchtime, I make a peanut butter sandwich and take it down the street so I can eat lunch with Alfonse. Then I go to the cove for a while and fall asleep in the warm midday sun by mistake and get a sunburned nose.

I hurry back to the house. The phone doesn't ring, but it's still early. At four, I get out the stroller and begin the half-hour walk down Main Street to Andrew's day care.

As I pass Golly Polly's ice cream, there's Shawn. I run over to him, holding the folded-up stroller across my chest. "Hi, Shawn."

Now he's circling me on his bike, riding so slow that his front tire is wobbling. "Hey! It's the birthday girl!"

"How did you know?"

"Danielle told me. Want an ice cream?" he says. "I didn't think I should get you another card in case you know who came flouncing into your bedroom again and read it. This you can eat! You can destroy the evidence."

"I don't want anything."

"Yes, you do."

He buys me a double dip with rainbow sprinkles. Then he rides in circles around me all the way to the Main Street intersection. He has to take the inland road home.

"Hi, Jasmyn," Andrew's day-care teacher says. "I want to show you something. Andrew, come here, honey. Watch this."

She sets Andrew on his feet behind the stroller, so he's holding the handles. All the babies pause to watch. Andrew grins a big drooly grin.

"Go on, Andrew," the teacher says. "You can do it."

Suddenly he takes two or three wobbly steps. Then plunk! He sits down.

"Andrew! You were walking! Oh, wow. What a big boy."

"He did that a couple of times today," the teacher says. "He's a big guy now."

"Wait till I tell Mom about you," I say. "She's going to call today. It's my birthday."

"Oh, congratulations," his teacher says. "See you tomorrow, Andrew."

We head up Main Street. Andrew holds his Binky close. He seems to have forgotten Mom. At first he said her name all the time, but now he doesn't. She sent a picture of herself in her desert uniform, but he wasn't interested. He just chewed it and Jake said there were chemicals on the paper and we had to take it away from him. Now it's posted on the refrigerator, half chewed, up high where he can't get it.

Andrew's birthday is coming up, too. He'll be one in October and I bet he'll be walking all over by then.

As we pass Golly Polly's, Andrew sees the kids with ice cream cones and reaches out his hand, twisting around in the stroller, opening and closing his fist, trying to grab some.

"We can't, Andrew. I didn't bring any money."

He cries in a halfhearted way, but then he settles down. I wonder what I'm going to feed him for dinner. Jake may have had his hours changed, but he still can't manage an organized grocery shopping trip.

Back at the house, I'm pawing through the refrigerator. There's corn from the Parnells, so I husk it. We could have just that. But I don't know if it's good for a baby. Scrambled eggs? No, I know: French toast. Andrew loves that. And I'll have French toast and corn both.

I poke around the kitchen, kind of uncertain how to start. I have to boil the corn in the big pan, I know that much. But where is it? I hunt through all the cabinets until I remember it's on a shelf on the cellar stairs.

After we eat, I clean the whole kitchen and run the dishwasher. Everything looks nice. The countertops are all wiped up and shiny. Then I sit on the back steps while Andrew digs in his sandpile next to the driveway.

Evenings are cool now. The sun is going down earlier and earlier. Sitting out here, I feel pretty good. I can see the ocean and the Parnells' garden and Alfonse, poking his nose around his rosebushes.

The sky grows darker. Finally I take Andrew into the bathroom and give him a bath. As usual, drying him off isn't easy. He scoots down the hall, buck naked, laughing hysterically, as I try to wrestle him into his pajamas. Afterward, I feel exhausted and throw myself down on the sofa. But at least I played with him and made him laugh a lot.

Now that he's asleep, I have no one to talk to. I have no idea where Jake is. What if he doesn't come back because of our fight? It's getting late; he should have been here ages ago. What will happen if Andrew and I are truly left alone? When Mom calls, should I tell her? Should I call Mrs. Roberge? If they know Jake ditched us, I might get sent to Japan for sure. There's a light on at the Parnells' and their pickup truck is in the driveway. So at least there's somebody around.

I'm dozing on the sofa when suddenly the phone rings. I'm jolted awake. It's nearly ten o'clock. I pounce on the phone.

"Mom! You called!"

"I wouldn't miss your birthday, sweetie. Sorry I'm late. There's been a communications problem here. A huge sandstorm. You wouldn't believe it, Jas. The wind whips the sand into everything and it stings. It gets in your clothes and eyes, even your mouth. And it was one hundred twenty-two degrees today. So, how was your birthday?"

I burst into tears. I've never lied to her before, and I guess I can't start now.

"Jasmyn, sweetie. What happened? What's wrong?"

"Nothing. I'm okay." How can I explain it in a three-minute phone call? It's so frustrating.

"Did you get any presents?"

"Yeah, I got corn from the Parnells and cupcakes from Mrs. Roberge. And you won't believe it. Andrew's walking. Well, a little. Today's the first time."

"Oh, wow. I wish I was there to see it. Is he growing, too?" Now her voice sounds shakier than mine.

"Yeah. He's growing. The little pumpkin man's growing."

"Cupcakes and corn, huh? Is Jake there?"

"Oh. Umm. No. He went someplace."

"To the Handy store?"

"No. Actually, he went someplace this morning."

"You mean you've been alone all day?"

"Yeah."

"Including now?"

"Yeah. Hey, Mom, I was wondering if you knew when you were coming home."

"Home? Oh, I don't know, Jas. I spent most of today passing out thousands of gallons of water and wiping sand out of my eyes."

"But, Mom, I need you to come home," I whisper.

"I know, honey. But I think the truth is that this is much bigger than I thought. I didn't understand right away what this was. I'm still not sure, and neither is anybody else. Listen, I want you to have a wonderful birthday. Can you think of one good thing?"

"Yeah. Andrew walked."

"Well, there you go. So. Does school start tomorrow?"

"Yeah. Well, we have a two-hour orientation for seventh grade."

"Good luck, okay?"

"Mom, is there a guy behind you waiting to use the phone?"

"Yep, there sure is. But he's not getting on until I'm done."

"Mom, what's connecting us?"

"You mean now? On the phone?"

"Yeah."

"A satellite. It bounces radio waves which . . . Oh, I don't know."

"I waited all day for you to call."

"I waited all day to call you."

"See you," I say.

"Love you," she says. "And listen, I'm going to call again in a few days so I can talk to Jake and make sure things are okay, all right?"

I fall asleep on the sofa by mistake. When Jake comes in, it's after midnight. I sit up with a strange sour taste in my mouth, and my eyelids feel sore. I rub them to get rid of it.

"Waiting up for me, huh?"

I can smell the cigarette smoke and alcohol on him from across the room.

"No. After Mom called, I fell asleep."

I get up and head for my room.

"Hey. Come back out here."

I'm scared now. I don't trust him after today—the way he acted this morning and then not coming home on time and not calling to tell me where he was. He's a grown-up, so he must realize that was a bad thing to do, and he did it anyway.

Knowing this is a heavy feeling, like a sigh that won't come out but sits in the top of your chest trapped by rocks. I won't turn my head toward Jake. I look out the darkened window.

"Hey! I just couldn't handle anything more today. Accusatory glares from you, diaper bags, no free time, no money. I know I'm not your mother, all right? So quit dishing out the blame. I'm doing the best I can, all right?"

"Well, so am I!"

I glare at him even though he said not to. He's really angry. But I have no idea what he means. I guess he's drunk.

Then he says more calmly, "The truth is, I forgot your birthday. Completely forgot it. I don't know what to get you. What am I supposed to get you? I don't know kids. I don't know anything about twelve-year-old girls. No. Wait. A dog or horse, probably. You want a horse?"

"Sure. I'll take a horse. A horse would be great."

"Yeah, well, you can't have one. We can't afford the hay."

In spite of myself, I have to smile a little. He's calmer now.

"Listen, Jas, I know I'm a little rough around the edges. Today I went to a bar after work, and you may have noticed, I didn't come back for quite a while. I guess a man's got to feel like he's always got a way out, always got an escape route if he wants one. We were playing cards, darts. And then a group of women from the factory came in. They sat down with us. We ordered some nachos."

I stare at the floor. My feet are there. My long and narrow feet that are going to carry me away from this place someday. If he has betrayed my mother or Andrew, I will kill him.

"And it started getting kind of late. At some point, I noticed this older guy watching me. He's just sitting there over by the bar. No drinks, no cigarettes. Nothing. He's watching me. Me. Leaning back in his seat. As though he's asking me, 'Well, what are you going to do? Ignore the dedication of a brave woman because it means you have to go home every day? Are you going to turn your back on her when she needs your support?' So, I got up. I laid my money on the table, said goodbye to everybody, and walked out. Now I'm here. I got no present for you other than the fact that I came back."

"Great. Thanks."

I get up and walk through the kitchen. I turn on the outside light. My ball is in the grass. A few dribbles to loosen up and I drive in for the layup. I'm going to practice until I drop in my tracks.

I won't stay here. I'm going to play basketball all the way through high school, and I'm going to go to a far-away college on a great big scholarship, and get out of Stroudwater forever. I don't want to end up like Jake, working in a factory warehouse for ten years by the time I'm thirty. Going to a bar afterward. Weak-minded. Not knowing right from wrong. Breathing smoke. That's not going to be my life.

I stand out there dribbling the ball. *Thunk, thunk, thunk.* It's well after midnight. I bounce the ball harder. I hope I wake up the whole world.

# 18

Wednesday morning is the orientation for junior high school. We get to meet our new teacher, Miss Powell. She's nice, a lot nicer than the other homeroom teacher, Mrs. Ornikowsky. We get assigned our lockers and our schedules. Because the school has so few kids, the seventh grade is divided according to who takes Spanish and who takes French. I chose French so I could be with Danielle.

I can't get my locker combination to work, and neither can Danielle. Shawn switches lockers so he can have the one next to me.

"Hey, how are your oxen doing?" I ask.

He smiles a huge smile, and I know I've made his day. "I've been really busy. Tomorrow the New England fairs start. I'm going down to Springfield, Massachusetts, for a few days."

"You're going to miss the first two days of school?"

"Yup. The oxen look gorgeous. My dad even put yellow pinstriping on the trailer. Everybody says my team's going to come in first."

"What do you mean first?"

"Well, you know, first place in New England."

"Wow, Shawn, that's great."

"Yeah. Too bad the principal doesn't think so. He's giving me two detentions. One for each day I miss. My dad is ripping."

"Hey, Shawn, I've been meaning to ask—is it okay if I go out to your house when you get back and see your oxen?"

"Sure," says Shawn. "It's more than okay."

Trying to open our lockers was the last thing we had to do for orientation. We head outside. Most of the kids are hanging around the high school parking lot, talking and chasing each other. Some are going over to Golly Polly's, which opens at eleven.

"You want to go get some ice cream?"

"Sure."

When Shawn and I turn away from the window with our cones, I see Danielle, Amy, and Bridget crossing the street together.

"Hi!" Danielle calls out as she hurries up to us. "Hi, Shawn."

"Hi! What's up?" I ask Danielle.

She blushes and avoids my eyes. "Nothing much. We just came for an ice cream cone." But I know they've been talking about me. She knows I know. Danielle wants to get everyone together. She thinks she can do that—by sharing cupcakes or being cheerful. She's pretty good at it, too.

I glance at Bridget and see she's looking at Shawn. I can sense that some rude cow joke is welling up inside her, but she doesn't dare say anything. I'd pound her is why. Her eyes meet mine. I give her a big, wide smile.

She looks away and moves forward in line with Amy.

"We might go to the mall later," Danielle says. "For school supplies. Want to come?"

"Yeah. I might. I need supplies, too, and new sneakers. Call me up, okay?"

Shawn and I sidle our way out of the crowd and stand under the streetlight, where the moths flicker when evening comes. I lick my cone all the way around to keep it from dripping. Shawn nudges me, sensing I'm far away.

"Worried about Bridget?" he asks.

"Huh? Oh, no."

"Worried about your mom?"

I guess he's starting to know me.

"Yeah," I say. "Yeah, I am."

With Jake on the early shift and school in session, I don't have to feed and bathe Andrew anymore. Now Jake has to do it, and he's the one who flops onto the sofa with the remote at eight o'clock. I get to walk home with the other kids and do my homework.

Since our big fight on my birthday, Jake and I speak, but only about essentials: cruise missiles, Apache helicopters, tanks, aircraft carriers—and dinner and schedules.

Late Friday afternoon, I'm sitting on the floor playing tickly-boo games with Andrew, when I notice there's a special report from Saudi Arabia on TV.

"Jake! Hey, Jake!" I sit up, staring.

*In a special bulletin, the Iraqis have announced that the child Stuart, as well as two hundred other foreign women and children, have been released. They have just arrived at London's Heathrow Airport. They are tired, frightened, and hungry, but otherwise unharmed. It is not yet known whether this signals a change in policy from Saddam Hussein.*

There's a video of the Reverend Jesse Jackson carrying Stuart in his arms. He's free!

"Hurray! Jake! Look! Look! He's leaving. Stuart's been set free! Did you know that? That's so cool! Yay, Stuart! You can go home!"

While I'm cheering and stomping, the phone rings. I forgot to tell Jake that Mom said she'd call again in a few days. I know it's Mom.

"Mom? Hi. Jake! It's Mom."

"How was school, Jas, you great big junior high kid?" Why does she sound so cheerful and phony? I'm going to ignore that and be normal.

"It's all right. My teachers are really nice. Fair time is next week. I have one big pumpkin picked out to enter in the vegetable competition. So, I mean, how are you? Are you too hot?"

"I'm fine. You just have to keep drinking water. Write me a letter, Jas."

"Another letter?"

"Yes, but I want to hear more from you next time."

"You do? No, you don't."

"Tell me about your teachers, tell me about Bridget."

"Even bad stuff?"

"Of course."

"You don't tell us bad stuff. Your letters sound like they were written by Chipper Chipmunk," I say bitterly.

"Hey, hey, cut it out." Jake takes the phone from me and turns off the sound of the TV guy telling us how cruise missiles can travel one thousand miles and still find their target and blow it up. I imagine a cartoon, tiny cigarette-shaped weapons flying into Iraq, blowing up a bus, people flying into the air. The thing is that in real life, they'd be dead. Dismembered and dead. I learned that on the news.

"Give me the phone back!" I yelp.

He waves me away. So I go into my bedroom, and for the second time, I listen in.

Mom's crying. "Jake, are you sure she's all right? She sounds so cold and distant," she's saying. "I'm afraid they'll never forgive me. I worry so, Jake."

"They're fine, Paula. Come on, now. Let's take it a week at a time. This week was back-to-school week. Next week is the fair. She's got a new friend, Shawn, who's showing a pair of oxen."

"Shawn Doucette. The boy who teased her last year?" Mom asks.

"Yeah. He seems like a nice kid."

"Andrew will be one soon. I won't be there for him." She's crying.

Gently, I put the receiver down. I had no idea this

might be harder for Mom than for me. I close my eyes and take a big, deep breath. My throat aches, I miss Mom so much.

A few minutes later, Jake calls down the hall, "I'm going to run down to the Handy store for a beer. You want anything with dinner? A soda?"

"Sure. A ginger ale."

"Be right back." I hear the door close.

I go into their bedroom and turn on the light. In the drawer of the nightstand I find Mom's latest letter.

*Dear Jake,*

*Nobody tells us what's going on even after weeks of waiting. We've pulled up stakes and moved closer to Kuwait several times. The air traffic in and out of the region is crazy. Twenty-four hours a day, transport planes are coming in from all over Europe. The buildup is massive. They must think Saddam has the power to blow us all away. With most of the basic supplies in, they've got everybody digging foxholes now that it's not so hot. Try digging a foxhole in the desert. Dry sand just falls back in the hole as soon as you turn your back on it. What a joke.*

*I'm on night watch now, too. The desert is freezing cold at night. I put on four layers of clothes, everything I have, and I still freeze. There I am, sitting in this foxhole with an M16 rifle for four hours with one guy. We both have to wear night vision goggles that cost $7,000 apiece. They turn everything*

145

*green. The stars out here are amazing, Jake. I wish I
had a little telescope or something. I worry so much
about you all at night. It hurts so much to have
missed Andrew's first steps. Does he miss me? Has he
forgotten me? You asked about the food in your letter.
Well, they have these dry meals called MRE, which in
army talk means Meals Ready to Eat. These things
make school lunches look terrific. They come in little
brown pouches—pork patty cat food, dry chicken
Styrofoam bits, brownie crumbled to dust, crushed
saltines. The best thing is the granola bar. We have
had dried-out chili for nine days in a row now.*

    *It looks to most of us like the big bosses are getting
ready for a massive air strike against the Iraqis at
some point, which is supposed to prevent any ground
fighting at all. Let's hope!! There are these new
weapons—smart weapons, Tomahawk cruise
missiles—that can be programmed to hit any target
at all, a bridge, a factory, whatever, from over a
thousand miles away. Send me a photo—anything—I
will cherish it.*

*Love, Paula*

I fold the letter carefully and put it back in the drawer.
I think about what I heard on the phone. I can't let her
go on thinking I hate her and am cold toward her. I still
feel dreadful about how I acted at the bus station when
she left.

I go to my room and write to my mother.

*Dear Mom,*

*Don't ever think that I'm not here waiting for you.
I'm here every day. I won't run away. Don't ever
think that I'm mad at you. I'm probably just mad at
the telephone. Don't ever think that Andrew and I
are all done with growing up and that you missed it.
We're kids and never get done with that. I'm sorry I
didn't say this at the bus station. I didn't know how
at the time. I love you. I love you. But don't ever go
away again.*

*Jas*

# 19

Seven o'clock comes and goes. I've already fed Andrew and eaten myself. Jake's not back yet. I watch out the front window. Our million-dollar view, Mom calls it. When the sun leaves, coldness quickly creeps out from under the fallen leaves, the beach stones, the splash of waves. The sunset is a faded red streak to the west.

" 'Be right back,' " I mutter angrily. Famous last words. How can I trust him?

Andrew is fussing because he needs a diaper change. I clean him up and give him a toasted bagel to chew on.

Suddenly the VW rattles into the driveway, headlights streaking up the kitchen wall. I hear the engine shut off. Jake comes in, whistling. I lay right into him. "Where were you?" I roar angrily. He tosses a little paper bag on the table.

"I was at the mall buying your birthday present," he says. "So back off, Bugaloo."

He brushes by me. But I don't even hear the birthday part, I'm so angry.

"No. I won't back off. You said a few minutes. You'd be gone a few minutes. But it's been nearly two hours. Haven't you ever heard of a telephone?" I ask.

"Yeah, I have. Is that what you want? A telephone call? Over something like that?"

"Yes. Yes, I do. So I'll know what's going on. Why can't you understand that? I lost both my parents, okay? My dad and my mom. They're gone. You're the only person left. So just call me." I'm crying now. "I have to know where you are."

So now he knows the raw truth. Jake knows how much I need him.

"Hey, Jas. I'm sorry. You're right. I should have called. You help out around the house and you're great with Andrew. I forget you're a kid sometimes, that's all." He gets the Kleenex box and leads me to the sofa.

"Here. I have something for you. Before you open it,

I want to say that I know I blew your birthday. And I'm really, really sorry. I was selfish beyond belief. Irresponsible. The whole bit. We were both under a lot of pressure, and I screwed up royally. So I got you something. A starting-over present."

He hands me the little bag. Inside is a velvet-covered jewelry box. It opens like a clam. The top snaps back, and the inside is lined with white satin. In the center is a silver ring inlaid with a braided design of turquoise. It's beautiful. It's my first really grown-up present.

"Wow, Jake. Thanks." I slide it on my finger. It fits.

Jake takes my hand. "I know I'll never be your dad. It's probably too late for that. But I want to be your friend. This is a friendship ring. I mean it about starting over, Jas. I'm not going to keep screwing up. You have to believe me. The ring is step one. But you have to start telling me what's going on with you, what you need. Otherwise I'm not gonna know."

I want to believe him, but it's hard to. I can't answer.

"Okay. So. What did you have for dinner?" he asks.

"Bagels."

"That's what we had for breakfast."

"I know."

He nods. "So I have to do better with dinner, huh?"

"That would be nice."

"I just bought some groceries. Why didn't you cook yourself a hamburger? Wait. Never mind. You want to see me do better? I'm gonna do better."

He pokes his head in the refrigerator. "How about I make you a cheeseburger and a big salad? Wait. Or eggs. Want me to make an omelette?"

"A cheeseburger sounds great."

While Jake cooks, I head for the hamper in the bathroom, trot downstairs, and gather the clothes from the dryer.

When I come back up, I'm worrying about something entirely new. If the war drags on for a whole year, maybe, or even longer, what will happen with Jake? Will he stay with us? And suddenly, I come to a stop. I decide right there, at the top of the stairs, while I'm still holding the plastic clothes hamper full of clean T-shirts for Andrew, my tights and basketball shorts, and Jake's pajamas, that there's only one way to go. Jake is all right. He may not be my father, but now he's a part of my family—forever, I hope.

In Maine, because we are near Canada and the ocean is so cold, a March afternoon means spring is still two solid months away. It will be weeks before brave, purple-streaked crocuses push their way into patches of sunlight near the warm foundations of people's houses, where the snow melts first.

In March, Mom's supply battalion is sent home, among the first troops leaving the Gulf. First to go, first to come back. We go to the bus station to get her.

At first we're all thrilled to be together, hugging and laughing, all except Andrew, who clings to Jake and hides his head. We come back from the bus station in an odd, bumping-into-one-another's-sentences-by-mistake kind of way.

At the house, our neighbors and friends are waving little American flags when we pull into the driveway, and they have strung yellow ribbons all around the front door, the mailbox, and our maple tree. Of course, the Parnells and the Roberges are there. Shawn comes with both of his parents. The O'Neills bring Alfonse. Even Bridget is there. Everybody is hugging Mom when she gets out of the car.

Shawn's mother is in the kitchen. She has set the table with a paper Stars and Stripes tablecloth left over from the Fourth of July. It looks great. After around half an hour, everybody goes home so we can be together.

We eat a big welcome-home Thanksgivingy sort of dinner, complete with cranberries and stuffing and apple pie—all brought by these friends and neighbors. Then, after dinner, Mom stares out the window at the ocean. "I missed this view so much while I was in the desert," she says.

Across the channel, Moorhead Island has the golden glow of late afternoon sun on it. A red buoy tilts and rocks in the water, marking the reef for the safe passage of bigger ships. The red color of it is deep and pure, as if it has just been washed. The air is sparkling clear.

"I'll clean up the kitchen," Jake says. "You probably want to get unpacked."

"Oh no, not right now. That can wait," Mom says.

"No. You know what? Jas, let's you and me go down to the cove. You want to?"

There's still plenty of icy, packed snow on the ground, especially along the edges of roads, and the breeze will be raw and cold. I hurry to get my boots. But I guess I kicked them to the bottom of the basement stairs. I race down and yank them on.

Going up, I see Mom at the top, smiling at me. She comes down a couple of steps and sits, taking my face in her hands. She rests her forehead on mine. "Thanks for your letters, Jas. They meant everything to me. I thought a lot about what you said. And I want you to know that if I ever get another call like that from the army, I won't leave. You have to trust me. I won't go. I'll stay here with you and Andrew."

"And probably Jake," I add.

She laughs. "Yeah, and probably Jake."

I lean my head on her shoulder, crying a little, but smiling too. She hands me a Kleenex. Then we hunt around for hats and mittens. And together we step outside.